W9-BLY-584

RIDE THE BUTTERFLIES

BACK TO SCHOOL WITH
DONALD DAVIS

L. E. SMOOT MEMORIAL LIBRARY
9533 KINGS HIGHWAY
KING GEORGE, VA 22485

AUGUST HOUSE PUBLISHERS, INC.
LITTLE ROCK

©1990, 1996, 2000 by Donald Davis, Storyteller, Inc.
All rights reserved. This book, or parts thereof, may not be reproduced
or publicly performed in any form without permission.

Published 2000 by August House Publishers, Inc.
P.O. Box 3223, Little Rock, Arkansas, 72203,
501-372-5450.

Printed in the United States of America

10 9 8 7 6 5 4 3 2 1

LIBRARY OF CONGRESS CATALOGING-IN-PUBLICATON DATA
Davis, Donald, 1944–
    Ride the butterflies : back to school with Donald Davis.
        p. cm.
    ISBN 0-87483-606-9 (pbk. : alk. paper)
    1. Davis, Donald, 1944—Childhood and youth.
    2. Authors, American—20th century—Biography.
    3. North Carolina—Social life and customs.
    4. School children—North Carolina.
    5. Schools—North Carolina. I. Title
PS3554.A93347 Z47 2000
813'.54—dc21
[B]   00-056911

Executive editor: Liz Parkhurst
Copyeditor: Laura Woodruff
Cover and book design: Joy Freeman

The paper used in this publication meets the minimum requirements
of the American National Standard for Information Sciences—
Permanence of Paper for Printed Library Materials, ANSI Z39.48–1984.

AUGUST HOUSE   PUBLISHERS   LITTLE ROCK

RIDE THE
BUTTERFLIES

L. E. SMOOT MEMORIAL LIBRARY
9533 KINGS HIGHWAY
KING GEORGE, VA 22485

CONTENTS

PREFACE

IT WAS THE FIRST DAY OF SCHOOL IN THE EIGHTH GRADE. THE YEAR WAS 1957. Our class, composed nearly completely of classmates who had been together throughout elementary school, had just met our first-ever male teacher, Mr. Roy Haupt.

"This is the eighth grade," Mr. Haupt told us. "This is your last chance to learn anything. Next year you have to go to high school and take courses. So...this is your last chance to get a useful education."

That year we learned to play bridge, to play chess, to read every kind of possible map he could come up with, to balance bank accounts, to amortize loans, to maintain imaginary investment accounts, to design and construct a weather station, to build a working model volcano, as well as all the more elementary things the school system required him to teach us.

Mr. Roy Haupt's stated philosophy was that he was an art teacher. When we asked him what that meant, he stared off into space and said, partly to us and partly to himself, "Art is anything that can take your mind to a place where your body can't go right now...and...if I can't make it art, it's not worth teaching!"

The stories in this book are possible because I was fortunate enough to have had a number of teachers, both in and out of school, who knew how to "teach art."

Occasionally someone who hears one of these "school stories" will say, "My, but you certainly had wonderful teachers." When I hear that, what I want to say is, "Wait a minute; when I add them up, from kindergarten through the extra-curriculars of high school, I think that

I had a total of thirty-three teachers in my primary and secondary life. The stories you read here are about fewer than a half-dozen of them!"

I don't say that, though, because if one has a half-dozen truly great teachers in a lifetime, this is enough to enable a learning student not only to survive but to prevail in the face of all the challenges life will most certainly bring.

I think of these stories as memory dusters. My hope is that, as you hear or read them, they will remind you of those few and special "teachers of art" who pulled you through and past all the rest and, in some cases, inspired you to become, in or out of the official classroom, "teachers of art" in your own way in your own world.

There are, in these stories, plenty of incidents of "kid trouble." This reality is there mainly to keep before us the truth that times and places may change, but "kid trouble" is an eternally guaranteed cornerstone of growth and education. I do not see reason, however, to model stories of teachers whose work has compounded that trouble, rather than enabling growth through it for good. That is the most basic reason you will not hear about all thirty-three of the paid professional educators with whom I served time.

I must admit that more of my teachers, though, do deserve to be remembered in story than are documented here. I'm working on it. So…if you are one of my old teachers and you don't read about yourself here, don't think automatically that you have been cast among the negatives. I probably just haven't gotten around to you yet!

Finally, let me leave you with another quotation from my eighth-grade year with Mr. Roy Haupt. Whenever whining sounds crept into our class for any reason, we soon knew what he was about to say to us: "Now remember, happiness is not a prize you win…happiness is a decision you make!"

From Mrs. Rosemary's teachings about death through Miss Daisy's surety that we could "ride the butterflies," to Stanley Easter's amazing ride, I salute, through story, all the teachers of every time and place who challenge their students daily to choose happiness!

—Donald Davis
Ocracoke Island
June 1, 2000

MRS. ROSEMARY

THERE WAS NO PUBLIC-SCHOOL KINDERGARTEN PROGRAM IN NORTH Carolina in the 1940s, but when I was five years old, instead of just staying at home, I attended Mrs. Rosemary's kindergarten.

Mrs. Rosemary's kindergarten was in the basement of the old Methodist Church in Sulpher Springs. Every day, on his way to work at the bank, Daddy took me there for my first experience of "school."

The church basement was actually half below and half above the ground, like so many church basements of the day. Daddy would take me to the top step, and then on my own, I would descend the six cement steps that took me into the wonderful new world created and shaped by Mrs. Rosemary.

The windows in the kindergarten room were high up on the basement walls, which were the first rough and randomly trowel-textured plaster walls I had ever seen, much less touched. I loved those walls. I could look at them and daydream just like watching the clouds in the springtime. I could see and feel the shapes of lions and birds and sailing ships. Why, I could stare at those walls and easily keep myself awake during nap time.

It was never very hot in the basement room. In the winter when it was really cold, our heat came from a gas heater that stood out from the wall on the side of the room away from the windows. The gas heater was covered by a cage made of chicken wire fastened to a metal framework for support.

When it got too cold, a condition determined by Mrs. Rosemary's count of how many of us were shaking at the same time, we would all assemble in front of the heater, get down on our knees on the floor, and watch her light the gas. We had no television in those days, and we would watch anything. Mrs. Rosemary would remove the protective screen, strike a big wooden match, and turn the gas handle. The hot blue flame would leap with a tramping sound from one end of the heater to the other. The whole class would applaud her success! Then she would carefully replace the protective cage, and we would huddle until we all warmed up.

Mrs. Rosemary was a strong, short little woman of indeterminate if mature vintage who was absolutely the same size all the way up and down from top to bottom. She could have worn her clothes front to back or front to front; clothing without sleeves she could have worn sideways...it would have been just the same.

Her glasses had gold earpieces that seemed to brad through the outer top corners of their frameless lenses, lenses that were slightly rounded on top but had three distinct sides on the bottom halves.

Mrs. Rosemary's hair looked like an old-fashioned bathing cap with flat, brown curls glued all over it. It looked for all the world like she could take it off, hang it on a big bedpost at night, and iron it all flat again before returning to school the next morning.

There were fifteen of us in the kindergarten class, and we *loved* Mrs. Rosemary.

Mrs. Rosemary could have taught television's Mr. Rogers. Mrs. Rosemary knew that the only way to stay even with a five-year-old is not by speeding up, but by slowing down. No matter what we started, there was never any time limit about when it had to be finished. "Why not?" she said. "It's kindergarten."

Almost every day we had rhythm band. Once rhythm band started, we could keep right on marching and making music just as long as we wanted to! When time for rhythm band was announced each day, I always tried to raise my hand just as fast as I could so that I wouldn't get stuck with the wood blocks. All the slow kids got stuck with the wood blocks, those flat blocks of wood covered with sandpaper that were supposed to make a musical sound when you rubbed them together. I thought that maybe I could never get mine to work because the sandpaper was worn out, but when I finally got a set with new sandpaper, they didn't work either.

If you were lucky (and quick), you might get to play the one triangle, the one tambourine, or the one set of cymbals made from flattened aluminum pot lids. But best of all was "the whip." The whip consisted of two thin, flat boards about two feet long. They were hinged together at the bottom and had handles like drawer pulls on the outside. If you opened them wide by the handles and then smacked them together as hard as you could, they made a crack you could hear for half a mile.

One specially selected person got to lead the rhythm band each day. There was a baton made from a fat dowel stick with glitter glued all over it and a rubber ball stuck on its bottom end. The leader marched in front while the rest of us followed, outdoors, all around the block where the church was. Around and around we marched, without limit, until we had had enough.

There was one bad boy in Mrs. Rosemary's class: Bobby Jensen. Bobby Jensen was so bad that he would spend an hour working his way around the room until he got in exactly the right place where he could see a girl's underwear! One day Bobby Jensen came to school and told us that his mother had read in the newspaper that a lion had escaped from the zoo in Atlanta and it was still on the loose. When we asked, "How far is Atlanta?" Bobby Jensen sneered, "Not very far!" He would have cheated at rhythm band if that were possible.

It was Bobby Jensen who first inspired me to worry about untimely death. I knew that things finally died when they got real old, but I had not ever noticed that sometimes life ends prematurely until Bobby Jensen came along.

The realization came one day when we were having free play

time outdoors. Davey Martin, Billy Stockwell, and I were in the sandbox, but Bobby Jensen was, as usual, playing alone. He was sitting on the sidewalk and had his sandal off his foot. He held it in his hand. A column of red ants was crossing the sidewalk single file. Just as my playmates and I, curious, walked close enough to notice the ants, Bobby Jensen came down on them with the sandal—*smack!*—and about six of them completely disappeared!

That night as I was trying to go to sleep I kept seeing that scene and thinking. What if somebody came along with a bigger sandal, then a *bigger* sandal, and then a BIGGER sandal? Finally somebody could come along with a sandal so big that they could go *smack* right on me, and I would just disappear! It was a terrible thought.

After a few weeks of kindergarten, Mrs. Rosemary announced that the coming Friday would be Pet Day and that we could all bring our pets to school for the day. This was the same week that the North Carolina State Fair was taking place in Raleigh, and Pet Day was to be our version of the state fair livestock show. I was not very happy about this whole idea because the only pet I had was the dead goldfish from the dime store, and it was buried in the flowerbed where the nasturtiums grew. I probably wouldn't even be able to find it. When I told Mama, she said, "Mrs. Welch has some kittens…why don't we just get you one?" That very afternoon we visited the Welches' house, and I came home with a yellow-black-white kitten whom I named Judy.

Judy went to school on Friday. Everyone loved her softness, and she even won the prize for Youngest Pet. She was so good that I thought she might have won the ribbon for Quietest Pet also, but that one went to a big earthworm that Billy Stockwell brought. Pet Day turned out to be a great day after all.

On that Sunday afternoon we got in the car to go to Grandmother's house. As Daddy started to back the car out of the driveway, we all heard a *ker-thunk* noise under the car. He stopped quickly. We got out in time to see Judy run out from under the car.

She went about ten yards before she fell over onto her side. We watched while her legs kept going in a running motion, then stopped. When I got to her, blood was coming out of her mouth. Instead of a trip to Grandmother's house, we had a Sunday afternoon cat funeral.

I tried to talk to Mama and Daddy about what had happened, but they didn't much listen and said silly things like, "Oh, it was just a cat," and "You can get another one." The next day I had to go to kindergarten and tell Mrs. Rosemary that my kitten had died—*"for no reason!"* I wailed.

Mrs. Rosemary listened carefully, then she gathered us all into a circle on the floor.

"Boys and girls," she began, "you have all heard about what happened to Hawk's kitten, Judy. He has told us that he believes that Judy died for no reason.

"Now, boys and girls, sometimes things do die. But nothing ever dies for no reason. If something dies, it is either because it got too hurt to get well, or too sick to get well, or, if you are really lucky, just plain too old to get well. That kitten just got too hurt to get well."

In my five-year-old mind that took care of everything. Mrs. Rosemary had listened, and she had given me a reason. My kitten had just been too hurt to get well. Now life made sense again after all.

Mrs. Rosemary's assistant at kindergarten was Mr. Rosemary.

Mr. Rosemary was tall and bald and definitely old. We were all afraid of him. He came to school at some time or another nearly every day, often quietly taking pictures with a little black box camera that he squinted down into the top of. Mrs. Rosemary told us that Mr. Rosemary had been gassed in the war and that he only had one lung.

Mr. Rosemary had a hole at the base of his throat that he breathed through. He wore a little bib over the hole, but when he bent down we could see it, and we couldn't escape the sound of his rattling breath. He talked with a little white plastic speaking tube, which he held with one end in his mouth and the other end against his throat. When he talked, he sounded like a creature from another planet.

One day Mr. Rosemary was at school, talking robot-talk with Mrs. Rosemary. All of us were huddled on the other side of the room, watching and listening. When he left, Mrs. Rosemary came over to us.

"Are you afraid of Mr. Rosemary, boys and girls?"

We all nodded in solemn unison. Davey Martin actually said, "Yes!" out loud.

She looked at us and thought for a moment. "Then just wait until tomorrow!" She smiled as she made the promise.

I could hardly sleep that night for fear of the unknown activity planned for the next day.

Mr. Rosemary was already at school when we got there the next morning. As soon as all fifteen of us had arrived, he got down on the floor with us and taught us how to mix up a recipe for finger paint. Then, to try out the paint, each one of us got to take a turn at finger-painting his bald head! While some of us were painting, the rest of us got to try out the little speaking tube to see if we could indeed sound like space creatures. We were never afraid of Mr. Rosemary again.

Mr. Rosemary made all of our toys. In the back of their house, he had a little shop where he had made all of the rhythm band instruments. He had also made our Maypole. The Maypole was mounted on a heavy base that looked to me a lot like a giant's Christmas tree holder. It had a wheel mounted on the top, to which were tied sixteen ribbons: one for each child and an extra one for Mrs. Rosemary. We could all go in one direction and the wheel would turn freely with us. We could face partners and "dip and dive" in opposite directions, and the blue and yellow ribbons braided themselves right down the pole, encasing it on the way.

The Maypole was such a great thing that Mrs. Rosemary introduced it to us in September, and after that we had May Day on the first day of each month. "Why waste a good Maypole?" Mrs. Rosemary said.

In fact, holidays in general were so important to Mrs. Rosemary that every Monday was a holiday. Before September was over we had already had Labor Day, Columbus Day, Halloween, and

Thanksgiving. In October it was Christmas, New Year's, Valentine's Day, and St. Patrick's Day. When we passed the Fourth of July, it wasn't even December yet, so we just started all over again. We had every holiday at least three times and some of them four. Why not? It was kindergarten, and we would never again get to have a full-scale holiday every week in all our lives.

Fridays were birthdays—over and over again. When the list ran out, we just started over. By the time the year was over, with only fifteen kids in the class, all of us had had three birthdays each. Why not?

Before his retirement, Mr. Rosemary had been an ice cream maker at the Fresh Meadow Dairy Company. When he retired he bought an old cream-colored Chevrolet Fresh Meadow Dairy panel truck, or maybe he just got to keep it. It had one small seat in the front just for the driver and was all empty with no seats in the back. Though faded, you could still see the green and black *Fresh Meadow* insignia on the side of the truck. The panel truck was our kindergarten field trip school bus.

Normally kindergarten got out at noon, but on Thursdays we were with the Rosemarys all day. Thursday was field trip day, and on many Thursdays we weren't delivered to our homes until dark.

We weren't very conscious of child safety back in those pre-seatbelt days. Mr. Rosemary simply opened the back door of the panel truck, and he and Mrs. Rosemary tossed all fifteen of us inside. We were so tightly packed in that there wasn't actually enough room for us to bounce around. Once we were loaded, Mrs. Rosemary would climb onto an upturned milk carton next to the front seat, and off we would go to explore the town and the countryside and to learn about the whole world around where we lived.

We took the same trips over and over again. We would go to the fire station, see all of the fire trucks, climb on the one old one we were allowed to touch, and beg to slide down the brass fireman's pole that came through the ceiling from the sleeping room above. We never got to do that.

We would go to the armory. The Sulpher Springs National Guard was a tank company, and they would let us climb all over the tanks. "A five-year-old can't hurt a tank," Sergeant Griswold at the armory told Mrs. Rosemary, "but they might get dirty!"

"They're already dirty!" she said, and let us climb all we wanted to.

We would sometimes go to the bank where Daddy worked and get to look at the big bags of money in the vault. He would even close us up in the vault and turn out the light so we could see how really dark it was in there when the big door was locked up.

We especially loved our field trips to the Fresh Meadow Dairy Company where Mr. Rosemary had once made ice cream. We would look through a glass window and watch the fast-moving and endless row of full milk bottles as they went under a machine that plugged and capped them so fast that we couldn't even see it happen. (Mr. Rosemary had told us that they moved at the rate of 120 a minute.) We loved to go back into the big, walk-in ice cream storage freezer and see how long we could stay there until we got so cold we had to run back outside, secretly hoping that Bobby Jensen got locked in. Before leaving the Fresh Meadow Dairy Company, we always got free Dixie Cups of ice cream and flat wooden spoons to eat it with.

Our favorite field trips, though, were those Thursdays when we got to go to the Rosemarys' house. It was a little rock house—our mama called it a "stone cottage." The roof shingles wrapped around the edges of its rounded eaves, giving the roof a thick, almost thatched look. In the back was the little workshop where Mr. Rosemary had made our toys and the rhythm band instruments.

The best thing of all about the Rosemarys' house, though, was that it had a rock and cement goldfish pond right in the front yard. I thought that the Rosemarys had to be very wealthy because I couldn't imagine how much that wonderful goldfish pond must have cost. It must have been so expensive that the Rosemarys couldn't afford to build a very big house with the money that was left over.

The goldfish pond was in the shade of some old oak trees. It was dark and shady, and the goldfish in it were very large. Mrs. Rosemary told us that they were tough. She said that when it got so cold in the wintertime that the goldfish pond froze, the goldfish would just sit right there and take it. (Later on I wondered, *What else could they have done?*) "Then," she went on, "when the ice thaws out, they just swim on away!"

Sometimes when we went to the Rosemarys' house, their one daughter, Ernestine, was there. She was maybe old enough to be in high school, and we liked her very much.

On one of those field trips to the Rosemarys' house we got a special treat. We got to change the water in the goldfish pond. Ernestine was our "special helper." She helped us dip the water out of the cement pond one bucketful at a time until it got so shallow that the big goldfish were flopping around. Then she waded into the low water with a bucket and caught each one of the fish in it.

After that we finished dipping out all of the water that we could. Then we formed a bucket line from a pump on the top of the Rosemarys' well and passed buckets of well water down the line until it was fresh and full again. It took all of the kindergarten day, but it seemed very important, and we were never bored for a single moment. We had, after all, had the very lives of those fish in our own hands.

There was only one thing about Mrs. Rosemary's class that I didn't like. I did not at all like the way she handled trouble. At home, when I had trouble with Joe-brother, all I had to do was to tell Mama on him, and that took care of things. The only problem with that plan was that if he had trouble with me, all *he* had to do was to tell Mama on me, and that also took care of that!

Mrs. Rosemary had a different plan. One day Bobby Jensen made me so mad in the sandbox that I just wanted to kill him. He had been picking and pushing all day. By the time he deliberately squashed a whole row of frog houses Billy Stockwell and I had worked hard to make in the damp sand and then said, "It was an *accident,"* I had just about had it. I went to Mrs. Rosemary and tried my best to tell on Bobby Jensen.

Mrs. Rosemary stopped me and wouldn't even let me finish telling. She said, "If you need to say something to Bobby, then you will have to tell him. I will sit with both of you and just listen if it will help." Then she made me talk to that "bad boy."

After that, Mrs. Rosemary had one of her little talks with all of us. We sat in a circle on the floor and she said, "Boys and girls, any time you have something important to tell someone, you never send a messenger. You must always tell them yourself. I do that with you, and all of you must do that with one another." I listened, but I still didn't much like it.

One day not long after that, Mrs. Rosemary had another woman with her when we all arrived at school in the morning.

"Boys and girls," she began, once we had all arrived, "let's come into our talking circle." The strange woman joined us on the floor. "Boys and girls," Mrs. Rosemary went on, "this is Mrs. Halley. She is going to be your teacher for the next four days. I know that you will take care of her and teach her how everything works in our class.

"I am going to have to be away from school for the next four days because, boys and girls, last night Mr. Rosemary died."

She could have sent someone else to tell us this, or just have had Mrs. Halley show up without any warning, but that would have broken her own rule about "important messages."

Before we even had a chance to feel sad or be upset, Mrs. Rosemary was talking again. "Now remember, boys and girls, what I told you. Nothing ever dies for no reason. If something dies it is either because it got too hurt to get well, or too sick to get well, or, if very lucky, just plain too old to get well. Do you remember what I told you about Mr. Rosemary's one lung? Well, boys and girls, he finally just got too sick to get well."

We all felt much better after that.

Mrs. Rosemary kissed each of us, and then she was gone for four days, just like she had told us. During one of those days we heard something going on upstairs above the kindergarten room in what all the grown-ups called "the big church." We could always tell when something was going on up there because the electric bellows that pumped air up to the organ was in a closet off our kindergarten room, and we could hear it every time it came on.

When we heard the sound of the organ pumping, Mrs. Halley told us that Mr. Rosemary's funeral was going on upstairs in the church while we were having kindergarten underneath in the basement. I thought later on that maybe it would have been a nice thing if the rhythm band had marched up there and played for the funeral, especially since Mr. Rosemary had invented so many of the instruments, but I didn't think of it in time. I guess that Mrs. Rosemary hadn't thought of it either, or surely she would have suggested the same thing.

The day after the funeral, Mrs. Rosemary was back.

We missed Mr. Rosemary. After he died, the field trips were not quite the same. Ernestine was old enough to drive the panel truck, but Mrs. Rosemary would not let her drive us on our field trips. Instead it took two and sometimes three parents' cars to haul the fifteen of us around.

Finally the year ended, and after the summer I started to "real school." Things were different in real school. There was no rhythm band. Everything we did had to be finished "on time." And we only got to celebrate holidays that the school board decided had really happened. Worst of all, we each got only one birthday, and since mine came in the summertime, I didn't even get that.

As the years passed and I got older and bigger, I began to forget about all of those things we had done in kindergarten. Once in a while, even after I had gone away to college and was just home visiting, Mama would turn to me and say: "Remember Mrs. Rosemary, your old kindergarten teacher? You know, I saw her in the grocery store this week…and she asked about you."

I thought, *So what? Is that all?* It never occurred to my adolescent self that Mrs. Rosemary might have had more than one class of kindergartners to ask about.

No matter where I went or what I did—college, graduate school, first job—each time I ventured back home, the story was always the same. A visit home could never be successfully completed unless some time or another Mama paused to say to me, "Oh, I almost forgot… I saw Mrs. Rosemary not long ago, and she asked about you!"

On one particular trip home—it must have been a dozen years after college—I realized that there had been no mention of Mrs. Rosemary. However, just about the time I realized that, Mother brought her up again. "Remember Mrs. Rosemary, your old kindergarten teacher? Well, she died about a week ago. Ernestine still lives over there at their little house. I saw Ernestine in the grocery store this week, and, she asked about you."

I started thinking about my year with Mrs. Rosemary, and before the afternoon was over, I found myself in the car going over to see if I could find Ernestine at home.

There was the little house. Small and stone, it *was* a cottage, with the thick, rounded eaves just as I remembered them. As I turned into the driveway, I could see Mr. Rosemary's old workshop there at the end of the driveway.

As I got out of the car, I was drawn not to the front door but straight into the oak shade of the front yard. There it was!

The goldfish pond. There were the giant, multi-colored goldfish lazing about in the shade. I stood there and visited the great-great-great-grandchildren of those old goldfish we had changed the water for all those years ago.

It was beside the fish pond that Ernestine found me. She had heard the car enter the driveway and had come out on the porch to see who was there. She knew me on the spot, and even after all those years I knew her too. Ernestine was the very image of Mrs. Rosemary, same size up and down from top to bottom, same flat-brown curls clinging close to her head.

We looked at the fish and visited by the fish pond. After a few minutes, Ernestine said, "Come inside. I was just going through some things you might want to see."

Inside, in the living room, Ernestine showed me a long bookshelf which was filled from end to end with what looked to me like note-book binders. She fingered the binders and counted them off, moving about two-thirds of the way down the shelf. Then she pulled one out. I realized then that this was a whole long shelf of photograph albums.

I followed Ernestine to the kitchen table with the one she had pulled out. As she placed it on the table I saw the cover. Hand-lettered, it read, *Hopes and Dreams—1949.* Looking back at the long shelf I realized that there had to be at least forty volumes of *Hopes and Dreams.* I also realized, with some embarrassment, that when my mama had through the years reported that "Mrs. Rosemary asked about you," that she had been keeping up with at least forty groups of little hopers and dreamers.

Ernestine placed the album on the kitchen table. As she opened it, we began to look at it together.

There were black and white photographs on the left-hand side of each page. (Now I remembered how Mr. Rosemary had always been taking pictures with that little black box camera, but I had never seen any of these photographs before now.)

There we were, the class of the 1948–49 year, pictured page after page. There were three whole pages of the rhythm band marching all around the church, all around the block. There we were, all clus-tered around the back of the Fresh Meadow panel truck. There we were, again, posing on the fire truck, dancing around the Maypole…the pages and the photographs went on and on.

On the right-hand side of each page we saw, not more photo-graphs, but newspaper clippings where Mrs. Rosemary had fol-lowed the lives of each of her students as far as the newspaper had kept up with them. Right there in Mrs. Rosemary's *Hopes and Dreams* book, I read about the time I made all A's in the third grade.

I read about my rock collection, which won the sixth grade science fair. I read about being in the high school band and about speaking at the Latin banquet in the twelfth grade. I read about my own high school and college graduations. The album was filled with newspaper clippings that my own mother hadn't even kept.

Ernestine and I looked, a page at a time, remembering pictured events and reading the newspaper clippings, all the way through the whole book. Then we were at the end.

There on the last page was Bobby Jensen. On a yellowed newspaper page was a picture of Bobby Jensen *wearing a Marine uniform!* The article told all about his joining the Marine Corps.

I pointed to the picture and then said to Ernestine, "I'm not surprised he ended up in the Marines. That Bobby Jensen, he was a *bad* boy!"

"Oh," she answered very politely, "Mother was always so proud of that picture. You see, she always said that when she first got Bobby Jensen he was the only real crybaby she ever had."

We looked back and forth through the photographs once again before I felt that it was time for me to go. It seemed to me that, sitting there with Ernestine, I was really getting to know her mother for the first time.

"I must go," I finally told her. "Thank you for this wonderful afternoon. You've helped me see a lot that I was too little to see way back then. I think that maybe I really met Mrs. Rosemary for the first time only today. I am really sorry that she is gone. Now that I know her…now I miss her! I'll bet that you miss her too."

"I do, of course," Ernestine answered, "but it's OK. You see, she probably never told all of you this because you were too little back then, but Mother always told me that nobody ever dies for no reason.

" 'If somebody dies,' she always said, 'it's because they were either too hurt to get well, or too sick to get well, or, if they were very careful and *very* lucky, just plain too old to get well.'

"I think that all of us who knew her were very, very lucky, because she got to be with us until she was just plain too old to get well."

WINNING AND LOSING

FOR SIX YEARS I HAD WAITED FOR THIS DAY TO ARRIVE. I WAS GOING to school!

Since the time of my earliest memories, Sunday mornings had been spent waiting for Daddy to get up. I waited because Joe-brother and I needed a "reader."

The Sunday *Asheville Citizen-Times* had arrived with its full-color comic section, and after Joe-brother and I fought over interpreting everything from "Maggie and Jiggs" to "Dick Tracy," we needed someone who could read to clear the whole matter up for us.

After six years of such Sunday mornings, the dream was coming true. I was going—Joe-brother was jealous—to Sulpher Springs School.

My personal plan was to learn to read first thing on the first day. After that, they could go ahead and teach me anything they wanted to.

It was Tuesday, the day after Labor Day. At 6:30 A.M. Mother got me up with orders to take a bath. "What do you mean 'take a bath'?" I asked her. "I take baths on Saturday night."

"Today is the first day of school," was her answer. "You've got to at least start out clean. We don't want any of the teachers at school to get you mixed up with any of those nasty little short-necked Rabbit Creek boys."

So I was scrubbed, then dressed in a brand-new pair of unwashed blue jeans which were so stiff I could barely move my knees. The blue jeans rubbed my skin very harshly at some uncomfortably tender places, and every time I tried to sit down, they were so stiff they tried to stand me up again. The outfit was topped off by a new shirt with a collar that felt like the edge of a tin can.

We all climbed into the blue Dodge, Joe-brother was left with the next neighbor, and Daddy drove Mother and me to Sulpher Springs School as he went on his way to work.

This was a school that looked like a school in a storybook. It was all red brick, with three sets of steps leading up the front to three sets of tall, white columns. The center steps led to the main entrance and on in to the principal's office. The other two sets of steps, I learned later, led to the auditorium and the cafeteria.

Mother and I went in the doors toward the office, but were quickly sent down a long hall of classrooms and into the auditorium for the assembling of new first graders.

I had never been in or even seen such a big room. It was bigger than the inside of our church. There were rows and rows and rows of wooden seats with curved backs and with seat bottoms which folded up and down making a loud "clunk" each time you dared move them. Each row was lettered and every single seat had a little oval-shaped metal plate, bearing the seat number, tacked to the seat back.

Mother and I took seats G-7 and G-8.

"Sounds like 'Bingo,'" I said, trying to make a joke. We were almost exactly in the center of our row, looking straight up at a stage which was closed off by a dark green curtain with "SSS" embroidered in big gold letters at the top.

I pointed to the letters. "What are those gold letters for?" I asked Mother in a whisper.

"Sulpher Springs School," she answered. "Just wait until you can read for yourself."

We were not alone. In the front of an auditorium that must hold the entire school, were on this day assembled more than a hundred new first graders. There were also more than another hundred mamas, and, I think, three daddies. Our row was packed. In fact, it seemed that at least the front half of the auditorium was almost completely full.

Finally the stage curtain began to open, operated by some powerful unseen hand. There, standing in center stage, was Mr. Lonnie Underhill. It would be several weeks before I heard that most of the kids at school secretly called him "Loony Lonnie."

With a deliberateness born of years of experience, Mr. Underhill began to welcome us to the first grade and tell us all the things we needed to know for success at Sulpher Springs School.

Mr. Underhill's speech went on and on. It was all about school spirit and behavior rules and school buses and how to pay for lunch in the cafeteria and how to buy school supplies in the office. There were rules about vaccinations and absences and on and on and on. It seemed like we had already been there all day.

At last, he began to introduce the first grade teachers.

First, there was Miss Caldwell. I should have known we were in for trouble when Mr. Underhill began by telling us the life story of Miss Caldwell's mother, who had taught him as a child and had put in years at Sulpher Springs before Miss Caldwell was even born.

"Miss Caldwell," he finally concluded, was just "born with teaching right in her blood." It was a good, long, substantial introduction and the first of four good, long, substantial introductions of first grade teachers we were to hear that day.

About this time I began slowly to make a very frightening discovery: suddenly I began to realize that for the first time in my entire life I was in a place in which I did not know where the bathroom was. Even if I had known, it would have done no good. Trapped in the very center of row G, there was absolutely no way out!

By this time most of us six-year-olds were getting wiggly. There was a growing amount of noise and seat squeaking going on throughout the auditorium.

Mr. Underhill finished his last introduction. I thought, *Maybe we'll get to go now.*

"Now children," he looked down at us over his glasses, "we still have a lot of housekeeping to take care of. I see, or rather I *hear*, that some of you are having trouble keeping your seats quiet. Let's stop now and have a few minutes of 'quiet seat drill.' "

For what seemed like the next twenty minutes, we practiced: standing up, folding our seats up so that they didn't make a sound, folding them down again, sitting down. Over and over and over again, until we were quiet enough to suit Mr. Underhill. The activity was also somewhat helpful, in that it took my attention off the bathroom emergency for awhile.

"Next, boys and girls," Mr. Underhill began as soon as we were seated quietly again, "we have to call the roll." With every name he called, the bathroom crisis got worse and worse until, by the time he was passing "Setzer...Smith...Summey..." I began to realize that I could not possibly be dry by the time we finally got out of this place.

I began to try every trick I could possibly think of to relieve the pain that was steadily increasing in my bladder. I gripped the wooden arms of the auditorium seats until my knuckles turned white, and it seemed that the bones might pop through the skin. I took in as much breath as I could hold, then held it as long as possible before quickly letting it all out and even more quickly grabbing another full breath. But, inside, I knew that I would never make it out of this place and to the bathroom in time.

In desperation, I tried to think of something good about all this. My mind was blank, until suddenly I got it! *I am wearing brand-new, dark blue, unfaded blue jeans. I won't look nearly as wet in these new dark blue jeans as I would in old, faded jeans!* That thought, helpful as it was, faded itself as the moment of truth closed in.

Mr. Underhill and the four first grade teachers had finished calling the roll. They had tried to find out the whereabouts of those who did not show up. They had added to the list the names of those present who hadn't signed up ahead of time. Finally, they had counted the names and divided by four and determined that "all students from Patricia Abernethy to Thomas Greene will be in Miss Caldwell's room." That's me! If we go now, I can make it!

But it was not to be so. It was time for Mr. Underhill's first-day-of-school principal speech. "Life," he began. (I was content just to learn to read on this first day...life could wait until later. He went on anyway.) "Life, boys and girls, is made up of two things: WINNING and LOSING." He was right, and I was about to lose right then! "The most important thing that you have to learn in school is that you do a lot more losing than winning. But, once in a while, boys and girls, you do get to win. And when that time finally comes, it is so good that you forget all about all the losing you did to get there."

The closing part of the speech was lost on me as I began my own version of losing—first a drop, then a trickle, then a little squirt. Then I thought, *If you're going to wet your pants, go ahead and do it right!* So I did!

Oh, what a comfort it is to accept defeat *positively*, to sit in the wet warmth of knowing that the crisis is past. I was certain that I would not have to go to the bathroom again for the rest of the week after this.

Besides, the new blue jeans had worked! Seated as I was when the accident happened, I looked completely dry in front. If I could slip out of here sideways, with my back to the wall, no one would ever even know.

The wooden floor of the big auditorium sloped from the back toward the front. I could see kids in front of me jump and punch one another as they looked down and pointed at the mysterious stream of water which was making its way, one row at a time, down the sloping floor and toward the opening in front of the stage.

I could see between the heads of rows A through F well enough to see the growing puddle that was building into a lake on the floor in front of the stage. Just as I was sure Mr. Underhill would step out to the edge of the stage, look down, and demand to know who that came from, he suddenly dismissed us and told our mothers to take us to our rooms.

The crowd was thick in the auditorium, and we were all so close together that I was sure no one would notice. As soon as we got into the hall, I walked sideways, with my back to the wall. Mother, busy talking with other mothers about "who got the best teachers," didn't even notice.

We were almost to Miss Caldwell's room. I was nearly certain that I was going to make it there and get seated before anyone discovered I was wet. Here, now, was the door to the room, opened outward into the hallway.

It was necessary to turn momentarily to go into Miss Caldwell's door. In that brief unguarded moment when my backside was not protected by the wall, a little ugly nasty six-year-old-girl voice, so loud everyone had to be able to hear her, said, "Look…that little boy wet his pants!"

I really thought I was going to die.

My only hope was, "If I live, I pray that she is not in my room, because she…*knows*…what happened!"

I was without luck. Her name, I was later to learn, was Carrie Boyd, one of the "A through GRs" making up Miss Caldwell's class. After we were all seated alphabetically, that same Carrie Boyd ended up in the next row, right beside me.

It was a long, long time before I ever knew exactly what Carrie Boyd looked like. I could no more have looked at her than I could talk with her. If I looked at her and she looked back at me, I would definitely die. Because…she…knew! I missed out on *everything* that happened on the right side of the room because I just couldn't look toward Carrie Boyd.

We didn't learn to read the first day, or even the first week. It was a great shock to me to gradually realize that the more I learned about reading, the longer it seemed it would take to actually learn.

As the year rolled on, I began to make friends in Miss Caldwell's class. There was Annie Bowen, who lived just outside the fence of the tannery where her father worked. We had to pass by the tannery if we walked from our house into town in Sulpher Springs.

The stink—Mother said we should call it an "odor"—was horrible. Daddy said nobody who worked at the tannery ever got sick, because germs couldn't live in that smell. In spite of living in such a stinking place, Annie Bowen was a small, sweet, black-haired girl.

(It seems almost strange that I should even *think* of a girl first when most of my time was spent with three particular boys. Perhaps it's because none of these boys were in Miss Caldwell's room, though we all lived on the same side of Sulpher Springs and were together on weekends and in the summer. The three were Freddie Patton, Red McElroy, and Rooster Loftis. Freddie lived closest to me, and Rooster lived right next to Red on Maple Creek. We were best friends.)

Miss Caldwell had a paddle. It was a red fly-back paddle, the kind that came from the dime store. It had once had a rubber ball attached to it by a long rubber band. No one I knew could actually ever get the ball to come back and hit the paddle more than once or maybe sometimes twice in a row at the most.

Miss Caldwell had collected the fly-back paddle from a former student along with a collection of marbles, squirt guns and a few broken pocket knives. She loved to wave it in the air and tell the story of Markie Leatherwood, who had dared try to knock a vase of flowers off her desk with the fly-back ball while Miss Caldwell was writing on the blackboard with her back turned.

"Markie hit the vase," the story always went, "but he missed the rubber fly-back ball when its rubber band ran out and it flew straight back toward his face.

"I heard the vase fall," she said, "and turned around just in time to see the red ball smack Markie right in the left eye…hard. While he was hollering about his eye, I lifted the fly-back paddle-ball, rubber band, and all.

L. E. SMOOT MEMORIAL LIBRARY
9533 KINGS HIGHWAY
KING GEORGE, VA 22485

"As you can see, I have it to this very day!"

The rubber band and ball had long since disappeared, and now only the paddle remained, a constant threat of corporal punishment, perched on the front edge of her desk.

The paddle was not, however, her favorite punishment. She greatly preferred what she called "a little session of 'ring-nose'." Convicted of a minor offense, the guilty parties would be marched to the blackboard. Each person to be punished would, in turn, stand in a line on tiptoe. Miss Caldwell would then draw a small chalk circle on the blackboard for each person. The chalk circle would be at the exact height to keep one's nose pressed into, if standing on tip-toe. The chalk circle would remain undisturbed only if the guilty party's nose never slipped—any mistakes resulted in a new ring and starting over. One fifteen-minute session of "ring nose" was more miserable than any two or three outright spankings.

As the year wore on, I gradually got to where I could look at Carrie Boyd. By Christmas I could speak to her and just after Easter I actually borrowed a pencil from her. By the time school let out on the last day of May, I was convinced that Carrie Boyd had actually forgotten all about what had happened on that first, terrible day of school—or perhaps she had never connected the wet boy with me.

The next year "everybody whose last name starts with 'A through GR,' Patricia Abernethy through Thomas Greene," ended up in Miss Ethel Swinburne's room. No one ever moved to Sulpher Springs, and so the old Caldwell bunch stayed all together for another year.

Miss Swinburne was a portly character, whose girth more than equaled her height. She was one who would never blow over in a hard wind, and she was frighteningly shorter than some second graders. She had a unique voice that sounded like she was talking through a jar full of marbles rattling under water. All the kids tried to imitate her, but no one ever came close.

She did not seem to walk, but rather to flow around the room.

There was absolutely no up-and-down movement about her. We overheard Mr. Underhill one day saying to another teacher (quietly, to be sure) that "when Miss Swinburne comes down the hall, she reminds me of a tugboat, low in the water and full steam ahead."

Seating was again to be alphabetical, and I was again seated next to Carrie Boyd for the year. It wasn't so bad, though. We had actually become fairly good friends by now.

Miss Swinburne also had a fly-back paddle, and she used it. She preferred swift justice to the prolonged agony of "ring nose." In her room, offenders quickly and frequently tasted the nip of the well-worn paddle.

One of the paddle's most frequent customers was Leon Conner. Leon had been educated in general disruption by a long line of older brothers, most of whom had spent significant periods of time at the Stonewall Jackson Training School for delinquent boys. Miss Swinburne had taught all of the Conner boys and so was doubly on the lookout for Leon. He never got away with anything.

The normal procedure for paddling was for four punishment assistants to be chosen. Miss Swinburne jokingly called them her "corporals." Their job was to hold the arms and legs of the offender while he bent over the teacher's desk, rear end in the air.

Girls were never paddled, except once when Nancy Brittain said a word "so ugly that it turned her into a boy."

Leon's mother never thought he got a fair shake. She periodically came to school to have screaming fits in Mr. Underhill's office about "that teacher who beat my baby." Mr. Underhill himself was once overheard after one of the screaming sessions confiding to Miss Swinburne that the boy's mother could use a little taste of fly-back herself!

Leon had learned screaming from his mother. It seemed to be his duty to scream as loudly as he could before, during, and after being paddled. He would yell, "She's killing me...she's killing me..." at the top of his lungs as soon as he was touched.

During one particularly bad week, Leon had been paddled three days in a row. On Thursday he brought a square piece of cornbread back to the room after lunch and crumbled it into Nancy Brittain's hair while Miss Swinburne's back was turned. He told us later he was just trying to get her to "say that word that turned her into a boy" again.

Nancy let out a scream of her own, and in less than a minute, the four corporals were assembled at Miss Swinburne's desk as she rolled up her sleeves and picked up the fly-back paddle.

Down went Leon, bent over the desk. Two of the corporals held his arms, and the other two held his legs. He was already screaming, before the first blow was ever struck, "She's killing me...she's killing me...!"

Miss Swinburne started paddling. Her normal pattern was five whacks at a time: two slow, followed by three fast. These five-whack sets continued until she decided the punishment was sufficient.

Down came the fly-back paddle on Leon's upturned rear end: *"Whack...whack...whackwhackwhack..."*

Then, without warning, it happened: on the recoil from the three fast whacks, the fly-back paddle handle slipped out of Miss Swinburne's hand, went flying in an arc above the room, and with a loud crash, broke through a window pane and disappeared.

With this extra excitement, Leon turned up the volume of his screaming, now shrieking, "She's *kiilllliiing* me..." at the absolute top of his voice.

This was Leon's fourth paddling of the week, and it happened that his mother, Mrs. Conner, had decided after the third that today would be a good day to come to school to scream at Mr. Underhill.

She was just stepping out of her car, an old rusty low-slung Mercury, when the paddle came crashing through the school window above her head and landed, with a scattering of broken glass, on the sidewalk exactly in front of her.

Through the broken window she could hear "her baby" screaming,

"She's killing me…" at the top of his voice.

Mrs. Conner's screaming session set a new record that day. Not only did it last all through the time all the classes were going to lunch, but also she was so *loud* that all the kids in school got to hear her as they passed through the hall on the way to the lunchroom. No one could, however, understand a word she said.

The next day Leon did not come to school. He was absent the entire next week. When he finally did reappear on the Monday after that, he was mysteriously in Mrs. Elmer's class. "How did a C get in the 'GU through M' class?" we all wondered. There was no answer.

If life was made up of winning and losing, like Mr. Underhill had said, we figured Leon had lost!

April and May are long months for second graders. The days were getting hotter and hotter, and summer vacation seemed an eternity away. We were getting more and more restless, and Miss Swinburne was having a harder and harder time keeping order in the class.

On one hot day, after a particularly noisy time in the lunchroom, we marched back to our classroom to endure the afternoon. Miss Swinburne got all of us to sit still and be quiet. The she stood up (as tall as she could) in front of the class and made one of her famous "Teacher Speeches."

"Boys and girls," she began in her wet-marble voice, "school is not out yet! We still have four weeks, two days, and if the clock is right, one hour and thirteen minutes to go before school is out.

"You are not animals! The kind of behavior that was displayed in the lunchroom today cannot be repeated. In fact, this entire class is going to have to completely settle down and get under control if we are to come to the end of this year with dignity and order.

"In particular, there has been entirely too much disruption of our classroom routine by an unceasing stream of students claiming to need to visit the restroom when there is absolutely nothing wrong with their bladders except spring fever!

"From now until the end of the year, there will be no more of this back-and-forth 'being excused' to run to the restroom during class. Now you will go, on your own, before school, at morning recess, at lunchtime, or wait until after school. No exceptions." End of speech, amen!

I had never had any problem the entire year until she made that speech. But as soon as she began to make it clear that we couldn't go if we needed to, I started needing to go so badly that I could see the first day of school beginning to recreate itself all over again. Just as Miss Swinburne said, "you can't," something way down inside of me said, "yes, you can...*and you will*...SOON!"

There was a big electric clock on the wall, right over the door. The clock was one of those with a red secondhand that went around each minute. I knew that second hand would have to go around seventy-three times (if Miss Swinburne's calculations were correct), before we would get out the door.

I would take a deep breath, look away from the clock, and hold my breath as long as I could. Then I would look back at the clock to see if the red secondhand had gone all the way around once. After about a half-dozen of these big breaths, I knew this method wasn't going to keep me dry. I just wasn't going to make it.

Was there anything good to think about? At first, all I could think about was Mr. Underhill making that old first-day-of-school speech: "Life is made up of winning and losing...and there's a lot more losing than winning." He was right—he knew it, Leon Conner knew it, I knew it, and Miss Swinburne knew it, too!

Then I had a good thought. During the summer before, some of the schoolrooms had been remodeled. In Miss Swinburne's room the old bolted-to-the-floor desks had been removed. After the floors were refinished, new light-colored oak desks were brought in. These new desks, with writing arms on the sides, had sculptured seat bottoms designed to fit second grade rear ends—they were sort of scooped out.

As I looked at the empty seat beside me, it seemed to me that it would probably hold at least a cup of water. The good thought was this: if my bladder gets any fuller, and if it won't hold, maybe I can let out just enough to ease off the pressure and the part I lose will all stay right there in that scooped out seat! Then I can make it until school's out, and no one will ever know what happened.

Miss Swinburne was spending the afternoon of each day in what she called "basic skills review." All during the time I was trying desperately to keep from flooding the room, she was in another world leading us in a phonetics review drill.

"Don't forget Mister 'T'," she went on. "Without Mr. 'T,' the clock couldn't go 'tic-tock.' Now, all together, let's say the name of the letter, and then review the sound it makes. Here we go: T…T…T…T…T."

As the whole class chanted "T…T…T…T…T…" that is exactly what I did. "T…T…T," a drop at a time until I was almost floating in the scooped out seat of the new oak desk.

Things seemed safe. I looked at the floor. It was all dry. I would just sit in this puddle after the bell rang until all the children were out of the room, then I'd slip out. No one would ever know!

Then, from the row next to me, the same little ugly nasty now-seven-year-old-girl voice, yes, Carrie Boyd, with her volume at its very highest setting, said: "There's water dripping out of your britches leg! HA, HA, HA!"

No conscious thought went into what happened next. The reaction her words inspired was much too fast for thought to have been involved. My right hand clenched itself tightly into a hard little fist and shot out—*smack!*—striking Carrie Boyd full force in the mouth.

The entire room was silent. In the moment before her scream cut the air, we heard a little "plunk," as one of her big front teeth fell out of her ugly mouth and landed, bloody, right in the middle of her desk top.

I never knew what happened next as Miss Swinburne had me by

both shoulders, up in the air and dripping. She glided with me all the way down the hall to Mr. Underhill's office.

After a short, private speech, which I didn't hear a single word of, I was deposited in a chair in the outer office where I stayed, stared at by everyone who came and went, until the bell finally rang and we all went home.

Joe-brother and I walked home. If he knew anything about what had happened, he at least had the good sense to be quiet about it.

Mother knew. I could tell the moment that I saw her that she knew. It was written all over her face as she stood there in the door waiting for us to get home.

I did her a favor and saved myself some time by going on to the maple tree in the back yard and breaking off a switch before I even went into the house. Without saying a word, she gave me a pretty good switching right through those wet britches. Then she said, "You ought to be ashamed of yourself. Now change your clothes and wait for your Daddy to get home."

Joe-brother stayed pretty far away from me for the rest of the day. He didn't seem to want any of my trouble to rub off on him merely by association.

Finally I heard the Dodge come in the driveway. Daddy was home. I stayed in the bedroom and thought to myself, *If he wants me, he can just come and get me!*

He did.

"I understand," he began, "that you had trouble at school today."

I nodded my head. "Go ahead and whip me and get it over with."

"I'm not going to whip you," he said. "I guess you've had enough of that. But I'll tell you what you're going to have to do. You're going to have to walk up to Carrie Boyd's house and apologize to her parents for knocking her tooth out."

"No!" I almost cried. "*Please* don't make me do that. Please just whip me and get it over with." I was almost frantic. "Please just whip me...*twice!* Whip me three times...*whip me every day for a week*. Please don't make me go up there."

"No," he said in a tone of voice that had absolutely no room for uncertainty in it. "You have to go up there and apologize."

The Boyds' house was less than a half-mile from ours, up Richland Road and off to the side above Miss Annie Macintosh's house. It took me two hours to walk up there. I would take a few steps, then stop to think about it for awhile. I was trembling, shaking, exuding sweat that felt like cold drops of pure blood popping out one at a time and running slowly down my back. My whole shirt was getting as wet as my pants had been at school earlier in the day.

At last I got to the Boyds' house. I knew exactly where they would be, and it was not in the house.

Mr. Boyd, Carrie's father, had learned to fly in the Second World War and had a yellow Piper Cub airplane which he kept and worked on in Burgie Welch's hay barn in a long field across the road from and below the house. I knew that if he were home, he would be there, working on the airplane. So, as if to prolong the agony even more, I went to the door of the house first.

Sure enough, no one was there. Afraid to go home without my mission accomplished, I started the long walk down and across to the hay barn.

One side of the big sliding door that closed the end of the barn stood pushed partially open. I knew the little airplane was inside and I knew the Boyds would be in there too.

As I started in the door, I saw Carrie's mother helping Mr. Boyd lift the wooden propeller from its shaft on the front of the airplane engine and carry it to a workbench against the wall. Carrie was playing with a kitten. She saw me, picked up the kitten, and disappeared into the back recesses of the barn.

Mr. Boyd was starting to sand the rough edge of the wooden propeller. He stopped when he saw me enter the barn. Both Mr. and Mrs. Boyd just stood there and looked at me as I walked slowly into their presence.

My knees would hardly hold, my chin quivered, my eyes filled with tears which would not quite run over, but made my vision blurry and unreal.

I stood before the Boyds for a long uncomfortable minute while they looked down at me and didn't say a word. I had never talked to either of them before in my entire life.

"I'm sorry," I finally began, almost whimpering. "I'm sorry that I knocked Carrie's tooth out." It all came pouring out as the tears ran over and poured down both cheeks. My nose even bubbled.

The Boyds didn't say a word. They just looked at one another, at me, at one another again.

Then, as if in slow motion, Mr. Boyd reached into his hip pocket and pulled out his wallet. I did not at all understand what was going on. Slowly he opened the wallet, looked inside, and took out one of the first real five dollar bills I had ever seen close-up in my life.

"That tooth," he was talking to me now, "that tooth was a baby tooth. It's been hanging there by a thread for two months. Carrie wouldn't let either one of us touch it. Thank you for finally getting that thing out!" He handed me the five dollar bill. The Boyds both smiled.

Suddenly I remembered Mr. Underhill's speech, and I knew that he was right. Life is made up of winning and losing, and like he said, "When you finally get to win, it's so good, you forget about all the losing you've done to get there."

MISS DAISY

IN THE FOURTH GRADE ALL THE "A THROUGH GRs" (STILL PATRICIA Abernethy through Thomas Greene, though Leon Conner had gone to Jackson Training School for good by now) ended up in Miss Daisy Rose Boring's class.

Miss Daisy was one of the six daughters of Mr. Robert Boring. Mr. Boring had started Boring's Hardware in 1909, and having no son to take over the business, had hired Daddy to work for him in 1924.

Sixteen years later Mr. Boring died, and the six sisters sold the store to Daddy, who still ran it as Boring's Hardware. That same year he married Mother, having waited, properly, until he could adequately support a wife and family.

Instead of entering the hardware business the six daughters had years before become school teachers…for life!

I had not had Miss Lily, who taught second grade at Sulpher Springs School. She taught the "GU through M" class.

Anyone who had one of the Boring sisters for any grade in school usually spent the next year wondering, "Will I get the next one?" They taught all the even-numbered grades (2, 4, 6, 8, 10, and senior English) at Sulpher Springs School. If your name fell just right in the alphabet, it was possible to receive half of your entire public education from the Boring sisters.

Mr. Robert, their father (we never heard anything about their mother), tried to give all of them botanical names. He did well through Miss Lily, Miss Pansy, and Miss Violet. He must have thought Miss Daisy Rose would be the last, for he used two flowers in naming her. (Perhaps he was convinced a boy would come next.) When two more girls appeared, he started on gemstones. The youngest were Miss Opal and Miss Pearl.

Miss Daisy had taught fourth grade for forty-one years. She was a tiny, frail-looking woman in her early sixties. Her bird-like appearance prompted all of us to begin our first day of school wondering whether that little old woman could really handle us. We had, after all, been at this for three years already. The "A through GRs" were a tough bunch!

As we were whispering and wondering, Miss Daisy was giving what she called "housekeeping" instructions to the class. This consisted of instructions on everything from how to use the pencil sharpener to where to hang your coat.

The door of the classroom was standing open to the hall, and a mouse, who had had the entire school to himself all summer and was now trying innocently to escape this first-day invasion of wild children, came into our room in search of a safe place of retreat.

The mouse, scared to death, made its way a few cautious steps and sniffs at a time along the base of the blackboard wall just behind Miss Daisy.

No one was watching Miss Daisy. Every eye in the classroom was on the mouse. All of us secretly knew that very soon Miss Daisy would realize that we were not watching her. *This will be the test,* I thought. *As soon as she turns to see what we're watching, we'll see what she's made of!*

In a few moments Miss Daisy caught on. She turned to see what we were staring at, and spotted the brown mouse just as it reached the corner of the room. She didn't make a sound.

Very quietly she opened the side drawer of her desk and took out two brown paper towels. We all watched, rapt, as the tiny woman slipped quietly toward the corner where the mouse was, squatted slowly to the floor, reached out, and caught the mouse in the brown paper towels.

She carried the mouse back to her desk (still in the towels), held it up in front of us. With one hand—*crrrunch*—crushed it to death and dropped it in the trash can!

Not a sound came from anyone in the room. ("Quiet as a mouse," I thought later.) After that, no one ever had any doubt about Miss Daisy's power; we listened to every word she said.

The whole course of the year was going to be great fun. As she described her plan to us, Miss Daisy was going to take us, without our ever leaving our room at Sulpher Springs School, on an imaginary trip around the world.

It was going to be a year of play. Each day we'd get out our maps and plan our travels. Then, with Miss Daisy's help, we'd go on our travels for the day.

She didn't pass out the spelling books. She didn't even pass out the arithmetic books. We were just going to play all year.

Our imaginary plan was this: we would get some of our parents to pretend to drive us to Atlanta in their cars. I was not sure about whether Daddy would take the blue Dodge. He didn't usually like to travel very far from home.

Once in Atlanta, our plan was to board the train. Miss Daisy told us all about it. It was "the wonderful Southern Crescent," with a dining car that had fresh-cut flowers and real sterling silver on the tables. We were all to ride the train to New Orleans.

After a day or two in New Orleans, we would load up on what Miss Daisy called a "tramp steamer," and steam away for South America.

The real truth was that Miss Daisy had never actually been out of Nantahala County in her life, except for four brief years some forty-one years in the past when she had ridden the train less than a hundred miles to Asheville Normal to learn to teach fourth grade. But for forty-one years she had sent away by mail and had ordered thousands and thousands and thousands of picture postcards. It was not possible for us to go anywhere on our imaginary travels, from a small town in Alabama to a temple garden in Japan, without Miss Daisy being able to dig down through her files of shoeboxes to finally come up with a postcard to show us what that place looked like.

Some of the cards were very old, with black-and-white pictures and ragged edges. We were fascinated by the old ones most of all.

As we went on our travels, we had to write down the names of all the places we visited and the things we saw: states, towns, geographical and historical sites, even crops and industries. We made long lists of famous people who had lived everywhere we went. We learned about all the things they had done.

All year long we worked at this without ever figuring out that Miss Daisy had us making up our own lists of spelling words. They were words that were much harder than those in the slender fourth-grade spelling books she had never bothered to pass out.

We also never figured out (or was it because we didn't want to admit it) that as we calculated how far we had traveled each day, how much money we spent for gasoline or food or tickets, how to change money from one country to another, and how to calculate latitude and longitude, we were doing arithmetic. Miss Daisy never called it that. We were just doing what you have to do to make your way around the world.

The class was divided into four "travel teams." Most of each morning was spent in planning each day's travels. Each team was given certain parts of the journey to take the class on. Miss Daisy would flit from team to team as we planned. She was informer, guide, questioner, always insisting that no matter how much we learned, she could always learn more in a day than we could!

Each afternoon, on a strictly alternating schedule, two of the four "travel teams" would take the class on their assigned part of the journey.

Miss Daisy explained it this way: "It takes twice as long to plan anything as it does to do it, so you get two days to plan before you present. 'Plan-plan-present, plan-plan-present,' that's the pattern we work on."

She called the first day of planning "rounding up" and the second day "closing in on it."

On Fridays, Miss Daisy did all the presenting herself, filling in our gaps and giving us what felt like a day off. This did help to make up for the tests, which also always came on Fridays.

We worked our way to Atlanta, then on to New Orleans, where we finally boarded a steamer named the "Aurelia" for our trip to South America.

The first day of sailing was very rough! One of the "travel teams" was charged with teaching us all about the ship we were sailing on. They decided it would be a good idea to list all the parts of the ship, and learning to spell those awful words with their apostrophes and unpronounced extra letters nearly made some of us seasick.

On Friday of that week we came to school very excited, wondering what Miss Daisy might have in store for us on her day to present. As we gathered in the room a boy named Lucius Grasty, one of the last of the GRs, came running into the room.

His head was stooped and he wore a wool knit toboggan. The homemade hat was pulled way down over his ears. He wouldn't take it off though it was still September, and not even beginning to get cold yet.

Lucius went straight to the back of the room, squatted in a corner, and refused to come out.

Miss Daisy came breezing into the room, took little notice of Lucius, and began the day.

"Today, children," she started in a hurry, "we cross the equator!"

That was fast, I thought.

"Have any of you ever crossed the equator?" she asked. We met the question with blank stares. We didn't even understand what she was talking about.

"Good," she went on, "because when we cross the equator we must have a big party for Neptune, King of the Deep."

As she kept talking about King Neptune, she went back into the cloak closet and started bringing out things that had been left there by kids at the end of school for forty-one years. Out she came with old coats, abandoned caps and hats, odd galoshes, umbrellas with broken ribs, even brooms and mops.

"On a ship, we have to work with what we have," she said as she began to dress us up for the party. Mop-heads became wigs, and we took off our shoes and socks like sailors. She pulled the shades way out from the windows and twisted them at an angle to make sails for the ship. We found a rope and took turns throwing one another overboard out the first floor window, and pulling each other back onto the ship again. She came up with a shaving mug from somewhere, lathered the boys up, and shaved them with a sword made from a yardstick.

"Some sailors even have their clothes run up the mast," she said. No one volunteered for that one!

"And some," she said, as she eased back through the room to where Lucius was still squatting in the floor (he had taken part in nothing), "some special sailors, like the captain's son on his first voyage, even have their heads shaved!"

As she spoke those words, she lifted Lucius's toboggan. There we saw it: he was the sailor whose head was shaved! We were all jealous. How did Lucius get to be the special one?

It was a long time later that I overheard Mother telling a friend about that day and learned that when Lucius had gone home the day before, his mother had found lice in his hair. She had shaved his head and washed it in kerosene to get rid of the lice. Miss Daisy had taken that little boy with the blistered head, and in a moment had transformed him into the hero of crossing the equator.

At last we made land in South America. After leaving the steamer, we visited our first city, Belim, where we discovered that everyone spoke not Spanish, but Portuguese. Then we hired small boats and guides to take us up the Amazon River.

Miss Daisy would stand in front of the classroom and say, "The Amazon is the longest river in the Americas. There are giant ferns there, ferns as big as trees. And butterflies—there are butterflies so big you could ride them…if you could catch one!"

Some of us who thought we were pretty smart would try to argue with her about the "longest river" idea. We would gather the maps and say, "Miss Daisy, what about the Mississippi and the Missouri put together? That's really just one river. They just got two names on it a long time ago. If you put all of it together, it's longer than the Amazon, isn't it?"

"Two names, two rivers," she replied. "The Amazon is the longest. Remember that—it will be on the test!"

No matter where we went after that (all the way down to the tip of South America, on an imaginary ice-breaker to the South Pole, up the Congo and down the Nile), the Amazon was always my favorite place.

That was because my big art project for the year was making a butterfly "so big you could ride on it."

Several months earlier my Uncle Floyd had tried to invent a flying machine. He had made a two-part framework out of copper tubing and the flat sides of orange crates. It was joined in the middle by a long piano hinge so that the wings could flap.

Once the basic construction was finished, he had glued what looked like two million white-leghorn feathers to both sides of the "wings." Finally he rigged a harness to the underside so that the wings could be strapped on his back and he could flap them with his arms.

When the glue was all dry, he carried the huge wings up a ladder to the roof of the front porch of his house.

He told us all about it later. "I was going to try a little test flight from the house out to that red maple tree," he said, "but a downdraft got me!"

He sprained his ankle crash-landing. He was lucky he hadn't broken his neck.

The lucky thing for me was that the crash didn't tear up the wings. As soon as the Friday after the art project assignments came, I started begging Daddy to take me to Uncle Floyd's. Once there, I started begging Uncle Floyd for the wings.

After taking off the harness straps to be sure that I couldn't try to fly with them, he gave me the wings for the foundation of my butterfly. We folded them by the piano hinge and took them home in the blue Dodge.

I went to work. The body was made out of some big mailing tubes with the ends stopped up. The head was a rubber ball, with pieces of coat hanger bent to the shape of antennae.

The big job was painting the wings. It took nearly all day Saturday. Yellow and green, blue and red, purple and orange, swirls and patterns, matching on both sides of both wings, until by the end of the day I had created a butterfly so big you could really ride on it.

The only problem was that with the body and all the paint I had used, the wings wouldn't flap by the piano hinge anymore. It took all day Sunday for the paint to dry.

On Monday morning Daddy said he would take Joe-brother and me to school in the blue Dodge. "I don't think that thing will go through the door of the school bus" was his excuse.

Now that the paint was dry and the wings were stiff, it wouldn't fit through the door of the Dodge either. So Daddy drove us to school very slowly, with the window rolled down, holding the big butterfly outside the window. Several times he pulled to the side of the road to let the cars pass which had backed up behind us as he drove slowly enough to keep the butterfly from taking off.

When I got to the classroom with the butterfly, Miss Daisy was thrilled! She fastened a wire to the butterfly's back, climbed on top of a desk in the middle of the room, and suspended the butterfly from one of the light fixtures.

For the remainder of the year it hung there, multicolored and beautiful, decorating the room and reminding us of the Amazon.

We traveled overland from the headwaters of the Amazon to the very tip of Cape Horn, took an icebreaker for a brief visit to a scientific research station on "that frozen, southernmost continent," then sailed to Cape Good Hope and up the west coast of Africa to the mouth of the Congo.

We hired small boats and guides to travel up the Congo. Miss Daisy showed us a postcard picture of logs being burned out to build dug-out canoes, and we were sure they were ours.

To our surprise, the Congo was not like the Amazon at all. Here we met shining black tribes ranging from Pygmies to Zulus, and we saw sharp-nosed crocodiles instead of alligators.

At the head of the Congo, we joined a safari which took us by Jeep and then on foot all the way to Victoria Falls, and on to the very beginning waters of the Nile.

As soon as the Nile was navigable, we built huge rafts, supplied them, and floated for days and days until we landed at last beside the pyramids.

After a short time of sailing on the Mediterranean, we landed for a visit to the brand-new country of Israel. It could have been an old country as far as our visit was concerned, because all the things we visited were, in Miss Daisy's words, "nearly two thousand important years old."

If the United States Supreme Court (the "Nine Old Men in Washington," Uncle Floyd called them) ever happened to come down to Sulpher Springs School to be sure that the separation of church and state was being properly maintained, they would have found Miss Daisy dutifully teaching us to spell the names of the leaders of the new nation of Israel and other important fourth-grade facts, such as the distance from Jerusalem to Cairo.

They never came, though, and so when school let out for Christmas holidays, Miss Daisy told us we could stay over in

Bethlehem while school was out. In spite of what the Supreme Court may or may not have seen had they been there, none of us was at all uncertain about why it was important to her that we go home for Christmas thinking of Bethlehem.

After Christmas, we again set sail on the Mediterranean, this time bound for Greece and then on to Europe.

While we were in Greece, one of the four "travel teams" was assigned to take us to the ancient Olympic games. This group decided that we really should have Olympic games of our own. Miss Daisy thought the idea was great.

"There is only one thing I must warn you about, boys and girls. In the old Olympic games the athletes competed with no clothes on." We all looked around the room and stared at one another.

Miss Daisy went on. "But since it's wintertime, I suppose we will have to wear clothing for our Olympics. Does anyone mind that?" It was as quiet in the room as when the mouse died.

On Friday (no tests this week) we all came to school with sheets to wrap over our clothes. It looked more like a ninth-grade Latin banquet than the Olympics, but we didn't care. Miss Daisy had even made laurel wreaths for the winners.

It was a day of great competition. Relays were run back and forth from one end of the playground to another, passing a baton made from an empty paper-towel roller. There was shot-put with wooden croquet balls, javelin throwing with sharp wooden tobacco sticks, and finally a marathon which went from the school yard out and all the way down Railroad Street, around a big oak tree at the post office, back behind the stores on Main Street, and ending at a finish line on the school ground just across the creek from where we had begun.

Running wrapped in a sheet was going to be difficult. We did as well as we could to tie the sheets up between the legs of our blue jeans so we could move more freely.

I wasn't much of a competitor in either the shot put or the javelin contests. Not being able to throw straight made it all but impossible to figure out just how far you could throw when a straight line was the object. Pauletta Donaldson won both these contests, but then she was the biggest kid in the fourth grade, boy or girl, and had longer arms than all the rest of us.

The relays were more even. Our team of four came in in second place and could have won if the baton hadn't been dropped twice (the winning team dropped theirs only once). At the very end of the day came the marathon.

The fastest down-and-out runner in the class was a tiny boy named Hallie Curtis. Everyone was pretty sure that Hallie could take the marathon with no competition.

Hallie was very small and had two cowlicks in his hair. One was over his right eye and the other near the crown of his head. His hair insisted on standing up in these two places, and Hallie couldn't stand it. It was hard enough being teased about being little. The cowlicks were too much.

Hallie would put lard on his hair in a futile attempt to make the wild spots lie down. It never worked for very long. The lard, however, vulnerable as it was to Hallie's body temperature, gradually ran down his face and neck. His shirt collar was always dark and greasy with melted hair-lard.

Hallie had the longest arms for his body of anyone we had ever seen. His hands seemed to dangle alongside his knees as he walked along. Hallie's special trick was that he could bend just a bit and run on all-fours, just like a greyhound or a whippet—though he looked more like a greasy, escaped, dressed-up baboon. It was simply true: Hallie Curtis, running on all four legs, could completely outrun any boy or girl in any grade at Sulpher Springs School.

Before the marathon started, everyone complained to Miss Daisy that Hallie's four-legged running was not fair. So, to be fair, Miss Daisy warned him, "Now, Hallie, no running on your hands. You have to run on two feet like everybody else does. Those old Greeks didn't run on four legs!"

Miss Daisy lined us up. "One for the money, two for the show, three to get ready, and four...to...GO!"

Off we went, sheets flapping, girls screaming, across the playground, then spread out a little now, through the schoolyard gate and down the side of the empty street which ran behind Main Street and along by the railroad tracks.

The first half of the race told nothing. The sprinters rushed ahead, then started to wear out as the whole column began the mid-point turn around the oak tree at the post office.

On the way back the race really settled down. There was one good solid group of runners in the middle, with a slowly growing assortment of stragglers stringing out behind.

Out in front of everybody else, the real race was between Hallie Curtis and Pauletta Donaldson. She was nearly a foot taller and ran with flailing arms and long, gangling paces. Hallie's little legs seemed to spin like eggbeaters. His individual short strides couldn't even be seen as separate steps at all.

When they entered the gate to the school-yard and poured on the heat for the finish line, Pauletta began to pull farther and farther ahead.

Hallie couldn't stand the thought of losing to a girl. He didn't care if Miss Daisy had said that he had to run on two legs. He dropped to all-fours, and looking like a greasy-headed dog wrapped in a sheet, began to close the gap as the two of them outran everyone else toward the finish line.

A little creek ran down the middle of the schoolyard, and the finish line was across this little creek from where we were coming back onto the playground from the post office. The last thing all the runners had to do before crossing the finish line was to jump the creek.

It wasn't a hard creek to jump. We jumped it every day during recess as a regular part of most games, but I had never seen Hallie jump it while running on all-fours like a dog.

As Hallie and Pauletta approached the creek, Hallie took the lead.

He was nearly twenty feet ahead of her when, with a great push of his hind legs, he took to the air, arms reaching out in front of him, then coming back to touch the ground as his legs moved forward for the next step.

Something happened. Hallie's legs seemed to tangle in midair so that he couldn't pull his knees up. Instead of sailing across the creek, he fell like a rock, flat on his belly, in the middle of the water.

Pauletta never missed a step. She jumped right across him, and with a look of certain pride on her face, crossed the finish line alone.

Later we learned what had happened. Hallie's nose was itching as he came across the playground field on all-fours. He tried to hold back a sneeze as long as he could, but just as he started to leave the ground for his great leap across the creek, the long-saved-up sneeze burst loose. The great escape of the held-back sneeze snapped Hallie's belt right in two, and his blue jeans fell down to his knees, where they tangled hopelessly with the sheet which was tied up between his knees.

The sheet did protect his modesty, but the tangle had brought him down in great agony of defeat. He had lost to a girl.

Pauletta was simply disgusting as she wore her laurel wreath for the rest of the entire day.

When we finished with Greece, we made a great circle through Europe and spent the rest of the springtime crossing Asia: China, Japan, down to New Zealand and Australia, then over the Pacific, past Pearl Harbor and on to Los Angeles.

The last month of the school year was a long imaginary train ride, not across the United States, but across North America, Canada to Mexico, until on the last day of May, there we were, right back in our classroom at Sulpher Springs School.

The next year the "A through GRs" got Mrs. Kinney for the fifth grade. Mother said Mrs. Kinney was very smart, that we were lucky to have her, but it seemed like a long year as she tried to teach us how interesting the Greeks and Romans were, straight out of the book.

I had none of Miss Daisy's sisters in later years, and gradually I forgot about her as the importance of growing up made the fourth grade unreal, unimportant, and further and further behind.

At least ten years passed. I had graduated from Sulpher Springs High School and been away from home and college for a couple of years when I came home to work for the summer.

My job for this particular summer was working as bus boy in the dining room of the Mountain Vale Inn. The Mountain Vale Inn was an old hotel that topped the hill above "Old Main Street." It was the kind of place where retired Floridians spent the entire summer, while residents of Sulpher Springs had still not learned to charge them Florida prices.

It was a place with a dining room, a place where local residents went out for evening meals and after church on Sunday.

We served supper each evening from five until eight o'clock.

One afternoon about four-thirty I was outside sweeping off the steps and the sidewalk to the dining room when an old two-tone brown LaSalle sedan pulled up into the parking side of the yard.

Though I had not seen it in years, I knew the ancient car well. With its double-spares on the back and its landau trim, there was not another car like it anywhere in Nantahala County.

The LaSalle belonged to the Boring sisters. It had been their father's last car, new when he died, and they had carefully kept it. More than twenty years later, they were still keeping it—and driving it, it seemed, all over Nantahala County.

Miss Lily was driving that day. She opened her door and got out. As she walked around the long nose of the LaSalle, the other front door opened, and Miss Opal got out. The two of them opened the back door, lifted something from the back seat, and began to walk side by side up the sidewalk to the dining room.

I looked more closely and saw that they had between them all that was left of my old Miss Daisy.

A tiny skin-and-bones figure, less than half, it seemed, of the tiny thing she had been more than a decade earlier when I was in the fourth grade. She was between them, with each holding an arm as they brought her up the walk, little toes barely touching the ground. They were taking her out to supper.

As soon as I recognized them, I hurried down the walk to meet them. Miss Lily recognized me at once and spoke to me. Then she turned to Miss Daisy and said, "Look, Daisy. Look! It's one of your little boys...all grown up."

Miss Daisy lifted her head, and it did turn toward me, but her eyes were colorless and blank and empty. Nobody in there. After a long moment, her head dropped back to her chest.

My curiosity asked for a response. It came from Miss Lily. "Daisy has had a stroke," she offered.

While I was thinking that perhaps they were pushing things a bit having her out too soon in this condition, I asked, "When did she have it?"

In unison they replied, "She's had it six years." Miss Lily continued, "She got it when she retired."

I stood aside and watched as they partly led, partly carried Miss Daisy up the steps and into the dining room for her supper.

Once inside, I tried to do my work without staring, but from time to time did glance to see Miss Lily and Miss Opal cutting up tiny bites on Miss Daisy's plate. They mashed green beans and bits of potato, then helped her swallow it with drinks from a small glass of milk.

Part of my job was to clear the dishes from tables as soon as people were finished with their meals so that the dessert tray could be brought to the table.

It looked like they were finished, so I rolled my dish cart to their table and began clearing things away as quickly as I could.

Suddenly, in the midst of my doing this job, I was paralyzed by the strange feeling of someone staring at me. I looked toward the feeling, and it was Miss Daisy.

She was staring straight at me, and her eyes were sparkling and clear. They were alive, and as blue as they had ever been.

Her lips began to quiver and then move, as from somewhere way down inside of her tiny body a thin, wispy ghost-of-a-voice came to life and softly said, straight to me, "The Amazon is the longest... there are butterflies here we can ride on..."

Then her eyes went blank, and her head dropped back to her chest.

I grabbed my dish cart and ran for the kitchen.

Mr. Gibbons, the old cook, was looking out of the kitchen door and muttering to himself, "Isn't it sad about poor Miss Daisy...isn't it sad."

No, it's not! I thought, but only to myself. *No, it's not sad.* Until a few moments ago I had thought the same thing, but now I felt as if I had made the greatest discovery in the world and had to find some way to explain it to Mr. Gibbons.

Then I remembered. "Mr. Gibbons," I said, "way back in Miss Daisy's room in the fourth grade sometimes we would get so full of learning new things and so tired of that traveling that we would look at her and say, 'Miss Daisy, why do we have to learn all these things?'" In memory, I could still see Miss Daisy holding her mouse-crushing fist high in the air, clenched, as she answered the question.

"She would say, 'Because, boys and girls...because! One of these days, when you grow up, you'll be able to go anywhere you want to. When that day comes, you simply must know where you are going!'"

"You see, it's not sad, Mr. Gibbons," I pleaded, returning to the present, "because I have seen that Miss Daisy is in a world in which she can go anywhere she wants to go, and she knows where she's going. Why, she can even ride the butterflies."

We looked back into the dining room, but they had finished and were gone. We heard the LaSalle whining from the driveway. I never saw Miss Daisy again.

EXPERIENCE

HIGH SCHOOL AT LAST! RED, FREDDIE, CHARLIE, AND I WERE ALL now in the ninth grade. While the entire seventh-through-twelfth grade classes at Sulpher Springs School shared the same buildings, there was a vast psychological and social difference between being in the eighth grade and being in the ninth grade. Eighth graders were junior high school *children.* Ninth graders were High School Students.

After eight years of public school education in Sulpher Springs, we were all experienced at dealing with teachers. We were ready and eager for the ninth grade. It took us some time to come to realize that the ninth grade was also ready for us.

One of the first things we noticed about the ninth grade was that all of the teachers were old. The oldest teacher we had ever had up to now had been Miss Daisy Rose Boring, back there in the fourth grade. Here in the ninth grade, all of the teachers looked as old as Miss Daisy had ever looked, and this entire old bunch seemed to be tough.

English was taught by Mrs. Amelia Harrison. Her class consisted of sentence diagramming, vocabulary drills, and manners lessons. Manners were very important to Mrs. Amelia, and every third day, alternating regularly with her other two priorities, we had manners lessons.

Each day of the world, she stood by the door as we entered the classroom. As we filed past her imposing presence, she held out a brown paper bag and sang a little song about "please leave your chewing gum and razors at the door," which she thought was very cute.

We were all supposed to drop our gum into that bag, though no one ever exactly figured out the part about the razors.

Every week we had a "chewing gum check," an examination of the underside of our desktops, to see if anyone with "bad manners" had actually slipped in with chewing gum and, horror of horrors, stuck it on the underside of his or her desktop.

One of the boys in our room was Billy "Bad Boy" Barker. Bad Boy happened to live down on Cold Ridge, and also, my mother said, was Leon Conner's first cousin. "He can't help it," she tried to explain, "their mothers just happened to be sisters."

Bad Boy, called this all his life by friend and foe alike, had what the teachers at school, after going to a workshop, began to call a "personality problem."

About seventeen years old now, Bad Boy would have quit school by now except that his mother, a real brute of a woman, didn't want his "personality problem" at home all day. So she made him stay in school.

Bad Boy was a long-time tobacco chewer, but he had been suspended from school for spitting in the floor and had learned to put his wad out when he got off the bus at school in the morning. His oral dependency was so strong, however, that he spent the rest of the day with a big wad of Juicy Fruit chewing gum in his mouth.

Mrs. Amelia should have been happy to get rid of the tobacco and let well enough alone, but she didn't. On the day of the first desk check, she found a half-dozen big wads of Juicy Fruit on the bottom of Bad Boy's desk.

"Why did you do it?" was her only question.

"The flavor give out in that Juicy Fruit, and I had to get rid of it," Bad Boy answered.

"That's not what I mean, and you know it!" she fired back. "Why did you dare come in my classroom with chewing gum in your mouth to start with?"

"Aw!" said Bad Boy. That was mostly all he *ever* had to say when he was asked a question.

She watched him like a hawk after that, doing everything but poking around in his mouth as he came into the room each day.

Bad Boy was lacking in many ways, but he was persistent. Even if he came in the door of the classroom empty-mouthed, it was not long until he had slipped a stick of Juicy Fruit into his mouth. He could sit, jaw slack and motionless, for minutes at a time—then chomp real fast whenever Mrs. Amelia turned to write on the board.

It had been so much trouble to have to chip and scrape the gum off his desk the first time he was caught that Bad Boy came up with a new solution for stale Juicy Fruit. Now when the flavor ran out, he just added a fresh stick to the wad and kept the whole thing in his mouth. His taste buds were so toughened by tobacco juice that he was often chewing a whole pack of Juicy Fruit by the time class was out.

As the year rolled on, Bad Boy grew bolder and bolder. Everyone in the room except Mrs. Amelia knew exactly what he was doing, and after a while the big seventeen-year-old ninth grader thought that even *she* probably knew but was just afraid to say or do anything about it.

The big day finally came. One day during vocabulary drill, the word under discussion by Mrs. Amelia was *hubris*. We couldn't find the word in the dictionary.

Mrs. Amelia said that didn't matter, because we needed to learn it anyway…especially in the ninth grade. She began to describe and define hubris as "fatal pride. The kind of pride which makes you truly believe that you are not like everyone else…the kind of pride which makes you feel that none of the normal laws of life apply to you…the kind of pride which brings you to a great fall in the end."

No one ever figured out what Bad Boy was thinking about on that day, but as Mrs. Amelia talked on about hubris, he very slowly began to chew, right there in front of her, what had to be a full five-stick wad of Juicy Fruit chewing gum.

Suddenly we realized that Mrs. Amelia, still talking, was looking straight at Bad Boy, unblinking, eyes open widely and set in a focused stare as she talked.

"Hubris is like," she went on, searching for an example, "it's like…it's like…well, it's like thinking"—she was on her feet now, and moving toward Bad Boy's desk—"you can chew gum out in the open in Mrs. Amelia Harrison's room and somehow get away with it."

Now she was face to face with Bad Boy. She held out her hand and with authority unmistakable even to a seventeen-year-old ninth grader, she said, "Spit it out…NOW!"

What happened next was so fast that it took a few seconds for all of us in the room to actually realize what had just taken place. Bad Boy did spit the huge wad of gum into Mrs. Amelia's outstretched hand. She, in one smooth move, stuck it right on the top of his head where, using the dictionary in her other hand, she smashed the whole huge wad down into his hair.

"Those who live by hubris," she kept talking as she walked back to her desk, "always get stuck in the end."

Mrs. Amelia had experience.

One of the bigger new things about High School was that we now had a chance to take a real foreign language. There was no choice about what to take. The one foreign language taught at Sulpher Springs High School was Latin. It was taught by Miss Vergilius Darwin, who had taught first and second year Latin for forty-six years.

We all called her "Miss V.D." behind her back.

Some days Miss Vergilius would tell us that she had started teaching Latin when it was still a living language. This was her joke, and she did not seem to think it funny at all when Charlie Summerow once asked her if she had ever had a date with Julius Caesar.

Miss V.D. was barely five feet tall and could have weighed no more than ninety-five pounds fully dressed. The main strength and power of at least ninety-four of her ninety-five pounds resided in the bent knuckle of the middle finger of her right hand.

She could grab a two-hundred-pound football player by the shirt, lift him out of his seat, sink that crooked knuckle into his chest and seem to stop his heart for twenty minutes. They rolled in the floor in pain.

One day during a grammar drill, Miss V.D. called on Big Tater McCracken to "conjugate 'carry,' present indicative, all three persons, singular and plural."

Big Tater was not only the first of the Rabbit Creek McCrackens ever to take Latin, but if he made it, he would be the first in his entire family ever to graduate from high school. He worked at Latin seriously and had just spent the entire weekend memorizing the very verb endings he was now being asked for. He was prepared.

There was only one problem. The model verb for this conjugation was the verb "to love," *amo,* and through the long weekend of Latin study, Big Tater had, a thousand times, repeated the conjugations to that verb: *"Amo, amas, ama...amamus, amatis, amant..."* He had it cold.

At this moment, however, an awful truth emerged. While all the verb endings had been memorized to perfection, Big Tater had forgotten to learn the new vocabulary words, one of which was the word *porto,* which meant "to carry."

Miss V.D. repeated the order. "Big Tater, I'm talking to you...conjugate 'to carry,' present indicative, all three persons, singular and plural."

Determined to get it right, especially since he knew all the verb endings, Big Tater sought desperately for the right word. Out of the corner of his mouth he whispered to Red McElroy, "What is it?...what is it?"

Red was the last person who wanted to get in trouble with Miss V.D. He shushed Big Tater, and then finally whispered back to him, "Damn if I know!"

That clue was all Big Tater needed, and he cut loose on the prize conjugation of the year: "To carry: *damifino, damifinas, damifinat...damifinamus, damifinatis, damifinant!*" He was proud to the end that he had done it.

"Whoooo!" Red threw his head back and hollered. "Damn-If-I-Knooow! Ha, ha, ha, ha!"

Miss Virgilius Darwin was on him in a flash, had him by the shirt and up in the air, then down onto the floor while she twisted that bent-auger finger into his chest.

All the breath went out of Red as Miss Darwin looked around the room and said, "Damn-if-you-better-try-that-again with Old V.D.!"

She had experience.

We all knew very soon, however, that experience was much more than a combination of old age and long tenure at school. This was obvious when we realized that our high school principal, in spite of his being principal for thirty-four years, was not a person of experience.

Before becoming principal, Mr. Walter Farlow had been the basketball coach, and as such had produced winning teams for several years. At some point along the way, the School Board decided that Coach Farlow would be a natural at being school principal, and so when old Mr. Wiggins retired, they put Coach Farlow in the office.

The mistake was soon realized, but it was too late, for his father-in-law was also chairman of the School Board.

No one was sure whether it was having to clean up and wear a suit and tie that did it, or realizing you just couldn't make teachers run laps around the gym if they didn't do what you wanted them to do. Whatever, the new job just didn't work.

Maybe he just couldn't function without his whistle.

When at our first assembly program Mr. Farlow gave us the school rules, we were slow to catch on. He began his recitation of each rule with the words, "I'd better not catch you..." and then went on to tell us what was prohibited.

It took us nearly a week to discover that that is exactly what he meant. He didn't say "don't do it"; he said, "I'd better not catch you," for he had absolutely no idea what he was going to do with any of us if he did catch us in some awful violation.

At every social activity, from sock hops to football games to real dances, Coach Farlow (as he was called forever) could be seen wandering the perimeter with a long, six-cell flashlight. The flashlight was not so he could see what we were doing, but so we could see him coming in time to stop so he wouldn't be forced to catch us.

Some of the teachers were heard to say, "He had ten good years of experience coaching basketball, but he's just been principal one year, thirty-four times!"

Coach Farlow did not have experience.

Back on the other end of the scale, the tenure and experience champion of all time at Sulpher Springs High School was Mrs. Ellen Birch Bryan.

Mrs. Birch Bryan, as she preferred to be called, since it "honored her dead father as well as her dead husband," was a huge, towering woman. Six feet tall, with big bones and broad shoulders, she wore her hair in a big gray pile on top of her head, which all went together to make her appear even taller.

Mrs. Birch Bryan was seventy-two years old and had taught typing, shorthand, business, and bookkeeping for fifty-one years.

"I'm not about to retire," she would say, which was no surprise to anyone at all at the time. With almost no retirement benefits and no mandatory retirement age, many teachers stayed in "for life."

"Why," she would say, "I've taught the principal. Not just this one, but the last three. I've taught the superintendent, I've taught every single member of the School Board, and I'm not afraid of the Supreme Court! Why should I stop teaching?"

Freddie, Red, Big Tater, Charlie, and I had Mrs. Birch Bryan for first-year typing during the last period of the day each day.

Every day, class began the same way it had for the past fifty years. We began with our finger exercises. "Now, boys and girls, hold up your hands and extend your fingers. Now, stretch, relax, stre-etch, rela-ax, stre-e-etch, rela-a-ax..."

After a few rounds of such digital calisthenics, we would all insert a sheet of paper, set our margins, and place our fingers on the home keys of the blank Underwood manual keyboards.

"It is now time for letter-by-letter dictation. Are you all ready? F...D...S...A...J...K...L...semi." Over and over again, we repeated that pattern until we all had it perfectly and as fast as Mrs. Birch Bryan could reel them off, first in order and then mixed up.

As the weeks went by, we added a letter at a time, gradually getting to "G" then "H," and finally on to the exotic fringes of the keyboard, including "P" and "Q" and "Z." We could do the entire alphabet now.

Once each week, there was a sacred time in Mrs. Birch Bryan's class. It came at the same time each week, as regularly as church came on Sunday mornings. It was the weekly "timed writing."

For the last ten minutes of the period on Fridays, we would type as fast as we could, copying a measured timed-writing selection, to determine our speed and grade for the week. Divide the total words typed by ten, and you got your words-per-minute weekly score.

Every mistake a person made subtracted one word per minute from the score, so that it was possible—several of us proved it—to come up scores like "minus seven words-per-minute," or once even "minus eleven words-per-minute." Sometimes after that I thought of just sitting still and not typing at all. At least I would end up even.

"Nothing, boys and girls, and I do mean absolutely *nothing,* must interfere with a timed writing. This is your grade, you are to stop typing for no reason until I tell you." This was the rule and the final word on timed writings.

We typed selections, old and yellowed, printed years earlier as advertising by typewriter companies who always pictured their newest machines at the top of the pages.

Some of these advertisements featured champion typists. Mrs. Birch Bryan's personal favorite was Mr. George Hossafield. He was pictured at the top of several of the timed-writing selections, seated at a now-ancient-looking glass-sided manual typewriter. He wore an eyeshade, and his sleeves were pushed up and held in place by elastic sleeve-holders.

The legend under the picture proclaimed that Mr. George Hossafield had attained his world championship status by averaging one hundred and forty-three words-per-minute over a period of time of one hour.

Mrs. Birch Bryan would hold up the sheet with his picture on it, tell us again what we already knew about his record-setting time, and say, "Aspire, students! Aspire! Some of you only have about a hundred and thirty words-per-minute to go and you'll catch him."

The selections to be typed were all about events that had been current in their time. Now, however, they were history. We typed about such things as Woodrow Wilson and the League of Nations, and even about Mrs. Coolidge redecorating the White House.

Mrs. Birch Bryan had a track clock with red and green stop and go buttons on the top of it. It was bigger and better than any timing device Coach Farlow had ever had when he was in the coaching business. This time clock was used solely for the purpose of timing the timed writings.

When we were all ready, she carefully wound the track clock. Then, as always, she left us with that last important admonition: "Remember, boys and girls, nothing…nothing must interfere with a timed writing. Are you ready? BEGIN!"

With that, she punched the green start button on the track clock, and for the next ten minutes we all typed just as fast as we possibly could.

To be sure that we learned to type through any kind of interference, Mrs. Birch Bryan would actually try to interrupt us while we typed. She would sneeze or cough loudly, blow her nose, open and close file cabinets, pop balloons, slam the door, and finally one day, she smashed a water glass in the sink. If anyone paused to glance up at her, she would pronounce loudly, "Nothing must interfere... nothing must interfere with your timed writing."

Within a few weeks, all of us could have typed through anything from a tornado to a train wreck.

By the end of the first six-weeks grading period, I was really beginning to become a typist, in spite of the discouraging scores on my timed writings. I actually thought about typing a paper for Mrs. Harrison's English class.

That thought vanished when report cards came out.

All of my grades were pretty much what I expected until it came to typing. Instead of a letter grade, there appeared the word "incomplete."

I didn't understand. There had not been a single day when I had missed school or typing class, the usual reason for "incompletes." I went to see Mrs. Birch Bryan to try to find out why I didn't get a real grade. She was ready for me.

"You are going to have to improve," she told me in her most formidable voice as she towered above me. She trembled as she spoke. "You are going to have to improve before I can give you an F. Yes, it would be an insult to the good, hard-working students who are earning good, solid, high Fs just to give you one for the kind of work you are doing. You must improve...you'll never catch Mr. Hossafield at this rate."

I was destroyed only briefly, however, as I very quickly learned that Red and Freddie also were going to have to improve in order to get an F.

On the next Friday, when it was time for the timed writing, I had an entirely new thought when, after the usual ritual, Mrs. Birch Bryan gave us the sacred reminder: "Remember, students, nothing must interfere with a timed writing."

Inspired by the realization that when you're already below F you don't have much to lose, I began to wonder—did I really think that nothing could interfere with Mrs. Birch Bryan herself during one of those timed writings?

After class, I raised the possibility with Red and Freddie and found out that they had been thinking about almost the same thing.

"Next Friday we'll find out," Red suggested.

On the next Thursday afternoon, we sneaked back to school and climbed in a window (we had taped it unlocked) of Mrs. Birch Bryan's room armed with a big roll of mason's twine.

The room was in an old building with tall windows. Each window had two shades mounted about halfway up the window frame. The top shade pulled up by a cord which ran through a roller at the top of the window. The bottom shade pulled down normally. Mrs. Birch Bryan never touched the shades. They were supposed to be fixed in a precise and unchangeable way: top shades all the way up, bottom shades one-third of the way down.

With the big ball of twine, we began tying on string to extend all the shade-pulls until we had a string from each coming around various heating pipes and meeting behind a radiator at the back of the room. After the ends were all tied together, enough tension was put on the cords to release the spring-locks of the shade rollers; then, by one string, the whole window-shade network was tied to the radiator pipe.

We were nervous all the next day about whether Mrs. Birch Bryan would discover the strings or not. She didn't.

Class opened as it usually did, from finger exercises through dictation and even some form-letter practice. Finally, after much instruction and preparation, we began the timed writing.

After waiting for about three minutes, Freddie Patton cut the main string.

There was a great noise all along the back of the room as sixteen window shades all rolled up so fast that most of them popped out of their brackets and fell on the students in the back row, unrolling all over everything.

Mrs. Birch Bryan simply bellowed, "Don't stop!" as if she had planned it that way. After school that day, she took the rest of the shades down and put them in the closet, and for the rest of the year we sat there in the afternoon sun, burning up.

"Let's try again," Freddie said a couple of weeks later. "I've got an idea."

Jean-ette Carlson was in our typing class. Jean-ette had cultivated a special talent. She could hold her breath until she fainted. We had seen her do it at school dances and picnics, and even once right behind the visiting team's bench at a basketball game. We each saved up a dollar, and we offered Jean-ette three dollars to faint during the next timed writing.

As soon as we started typing, Jean-ette began to hold her breath. It seemed like it took her five minutes until, beet-red, she fell out of her chair and into the floor right in front of Mrs. Birch Bryan.

Mrs. Birch Bryan simply folded her arms and looked the other way. "Nothing interferes," she whispered to herself. Jean-ette had to come back to life all on her own without any help! We could not ever get her to faint again after that.

We were beginning to realize that it was not going to be as easy to "interfere" with Mrs. Birch Bryan as we had first thought. Almost every day we spent some time trying to come up with a plan that might work.

Bad Boy Barker had study hall in the library while we were in typing class, which really meant that he could usually wander all over the school wherever he wanted to during that hour.

We saved three more dollars, plus an extra dollar for what Bad

Boy called "expenses," and paid him to acquire a cherry bomb (he seemed to have sources for such things) and to throw it into the room during a timed writing.

He did.

The only result was that before the next Friday came around, Mrs. Birch Bryan had installed a padlock and hasp on the inside of the door, and now, as part of getting ready for our timed writing, she locked us in! This really was going to be hard.

It was a very simple trick that finally did produce results. Without even planning anything in advance, Red happened to come to school the next Friday with a coil of transparent fishing line in his pocket.

While Mrs. Birch Bryan was shooing students out of the hall at class change time, he casually tied one end of the fishing line to a leg of her big oak teacher's chair. From there he ran the line through a drawer pull on the file cabinet at the end of the room and back under the front row of typing tables and tied it to his desk.

She never saw it at all.

We had class as usual: finger exercises, then F...D...S...A all the way up to Q by now, a long series of form-letters to type, and then, at last, the timed writing.

Mrs. Birch Bryan passed out the yellowed sheets. Today's selection was entitled "President Harding dies in California." She told us again about George Hossafield's record and admonished us to aspire. She wound up the track clock, and then she said it: "Remember students, nothing interferes with a timed writing! Are you ready? BEGIN!"

When Mrs. Birch Bryan pushed the green button on the track clock, Red McElroy pulled on his end of the fishing line.

The entire class was trying to type about poor President Harding's mysterious death while at the same time every eye in the room was watching Mrs. Birch Bryan as she slowly sat down toward a chair that wasn't there. Red had not, however, pulled the string quite far enough, and about four inches of Mrs. Birch Bryan's broadest self tried to sit on a four-inch side edge of the almost-absent chair.

Suddenly the chair popped sideways out from under her like a giant tiddly-wink, flew through the air, and crashed into the file cabinet, while Mrs. Birch Bryan hit the floor not once, but twice.

She sat smack on the floor, hard, bounced, straightened out, then landed flat on her back with her head making a loud *cra-a-ck* against the floor.

The entire room was silent, every typewriter dead still. We thought we had killed her! Sweat broke out in my armpits until they ached, and I could see Red's face flushing.

Then we heard a sound. It started like a groan or a whisper, but then, siren-like, it raised itself to fill the room.

"Don't stop!…Don't stop…" It was Mrs. Birch Bryan, flat on her back and bellowing at the ceiling. "Nothing must interfere with a timed writing."

We gave up on trying after that. Though some future typist might indeed catch Mr. Hossafield, Mrs. Birch Bryan, with a fifty-one-year head start, was clearly out of our class.

STANLEY EASTER

UNTIL THE EARLY 1980s, NORTH CAROLINA—AND MANY OTHER largely rural states—employed high school students as school bus drivers. Thousands of boys and girls all over the state were safely transported to school each day by drivers who were sixteen, seventeen, at most, eighteen years old. Then, out of fears spawned by a new era of litigation as an American pastime, the student driver era ended, and only adults were employed to pilot the big buses—now yellow, a dilution of their former orange—to and from school.

Actually, the new plan brought a great loss. When students drove, the safety record was very good. Driving a bus was a great honor in the 1950s and 1960s, and it paid well for a part-time job. It was hard to find a responsible adult who would take such a part-time job and even begin to do it as well as a student.

I spent my last two years at Sulpher Springs High School as a Nantahala County, North Carolina, school bus driver. It is impossible for me to remember a time when I didn't know how to drive. When you grow up in a rural area with tractors and trucks and Jeeps on farms everywhere, you just end up crawling up on them, sitting in laps of uncles, grandfathers, and fathers, and eventually driving before you even realize that you have learned anything. I remember turning the car around in the driveway at Plott Creek before we moved from there, before I was twelve years old. I remember that Joe and I both begged to drive down the farm roads whenever we went to visit our grandparents or aunts and uncles. Knowing how to drive was a very natural thing.

On the day of my sixteenth birthday, June 1, 1959, I drove Mama to town—she had to ride with me to make it legal for me to drive there with a learner's permit—and took the test for my driver's license. It was no trouble at all. I knew the answers to all the questions on the written test and I had been for years doing all of the things the examiner had me do for the road test. I was now a licensed driver, which meant that I could do on the paved public roads what I had been practicing on the farm and country lanes.

One month later, on the day after the Fourth of July, I went to the high school and started taking the two-week course to get my school bus driver's license. It had not been a long-term plan of mine to do this. It was Davey Martin who suggested it. He had called to tell me he was going to get his bus license and suggest that maybe we could both do it. So it was on the spur of the moment that the two of us met Mr. Joe Bennett and signed up to be bus drivers.

We were trained in groups of four. Besides Davey and me, Bobby Jensen, the terror of kindergarten and Boy Scout camp, was in our group. The fourth member of the team turned out to be the first black person I had ever met or even seen up close in my life: Stanley Easter.

The entire black population of Nantahala County was about five percent of a total of less than twenty thousand. That meant that the number of black school-age children in the entire county added up to less than two hundred, a number spread through twelve grades that totaled less than the consolidated white high school graduating class. Somehow the few black people I had had exposure to were either small children or old people. It was almost a shock to see someone exactly my own age who was black!

Stanley Easter was to be one fourth of our bus driving team, this integrated training being the briefest first step toward eventual desegregation of all levels of public education, which was not to be achieved for another half dozen years to come.

All through the years, Nantahala County had practiced busing—not to overcome, but to preserve segregation. Black children were bused from wherever they lived, all over the county, to a single black school that was located about ten miles outside Sulpher Springs, in the rural community of Pigeon River. There were black children who lived right across the street from Sulpher Springs Elementary School who were picked up there and bused the ten miles to their "own" school.

I realized that while Stanley Easter was going to be trained to drive school buses with the other three of us, he would never, in my public school lifetime, be driving either the same buses or hauling the same children I was to haul.

Right from the start, it was Bobby Jensen who was the outsider in our group of four. Davey and Stanley and I started to become great friends. It seemed a shame that it was to be a two-week friendship only.

Actually, his color was not Stanley Easter's only noticeable difference from me. He had the biggest biceps I had ever seen. Stanley had learned to drive the same way that Davey and I had—early in life and on the farm. We found out that his daddy had spent his life as a dairyman on a farm belonging to the Smathers family below Pigeon River. Stanley had driven tractors and trucks of every shape and size, not for fun, but because he had been working long and hard for as long as he could remember. He told us that he got his big muscles from throwing hay bales from the truck to the hayloft, and if that wasn't enough, he bench-pressed calves just for the fun of it!

On the other hand, Bobby Jensen could hardly drive a car, let alone a school bus. He was a pure town boy, who had had to take driver's training just to get his driver's license to begin with.

During the classroom part of the course, before we hit the road, Mr. Joe Bennett had told us again and again that more school bus accidents were caused by dogs than by anything else in the world.

He said that most dogs just couldn't resist chasing the big orange buses and that out of nowhere a dog of any shape or size was liable to come into the road behind and often in front of a moving bus.

The problem was that, just like car drivers, the bus driver's first tendency was to swerve so as to not run over the dog. The difference was that, with a big heavy bus, all loaded with loose children, if you swerved, the children would shift like a load of cattle, and the bus, now unbalanced and out of control, often turned over or at least went off the road.

"Go for the dog!" Mr. Bennett advised. "If a dog runs out in the road in front of you, just go for it! It won't hurt the school bus. It's a whole lot more important to keep your children safe than to save a dog's life, so, if one runs out in front of you, just grip the wheel, grit your teeth, and go for it!"

Two days into road training, Bobby Jensen drove the bus for the first time. We were driving over all of the school bus routes in Nantahala County so that we would be tried out on every actual place where a bus might have to go. On the second day we were in the north end of the county, and Bobby was driving about twenty-five miles an hour on a flat, gravel road that ran alongside a long, equally flat corn field. The July corn was mostly full by now and higher than our heads.

Up ahead, there was a break in the cornfield where a small frame house sat, close by the side of the road. Just as we got to the edge of the yard, a mongrel hound dog came to life from under the front porch and headed toward the school bus. Bobby, remembering Mr. Bennett's talk on dogs, took his advice and decided to "go for it."

Before any of us, including Mr. Bennett, had time to react, Bobby had turned the wheel and headed for the dog. In the seconds it took for Mr. Bennett to realize what was happening, dive for the dashboard, and cut off the ignition switch, Bobby had followed the dog out of the road, across the corner of the small yard, and had plowed the big, orange vehicle two bus lengths into the soft, green cornfield.

During those same seconds, Stanley Easter had turned white, I had almost wet my pants, Davey Martin was on his back on the floor laughing his head off, and the hound had safely escaped back under the porch of the house. Mr. Bennett couldn't talk. He just gazed up from the floor of the bus and *looked* at Bobby!

"What'sa matter, Coach?" Bobby said, almost offhandedly. "The bus didn't turn over. Hey, I would've saved the children *and* the dog!"

It seemed to me that the worst part of the whole disaster for Mr. Bennett was that he had to go up to the very house the dog came from, admit that he was the bus-driving teacher, and ask to use the telephone to call the bus garage so that the tow truck could come and pull the bus backwards out of the soft dirt of the July cornfield we had mired up in.

We all heard Mr. Bennett talking to the tow truck driver: "If I were closer to retirement, I'd just leave the damn thing in there and go home. I never have had a day to end like this in my life!"

Needless to say, Bobby Jensen was out of the bus-driving program.

So now our class was down to three, which meant that each of us got to drive more than before Bobby dogged out on us. Since the three of us already had a lot of experience driving big farm trucks which, if not as long, were certainly wider than the school bus, we spent most of our time just learning all of the routes in Nantahala County, while Mr. Bennett read and worked the crossword puzzle in the daily Asheville newspaper.

The driving part of the course lasted two full weeks, which gave us a lot of time to learn about each other. We found out from Stanley that he was just as scared of girls as we were, that he was as scared of his mama as I was of mine, and that, even though he played football for the Pigeon Eagles, he liked the rest of school a whole lot better than he liked football.

I told Daddy about him, including Stanley's hopes of going to college. Daddy told me that if Stanley was really a good football player, he might get to go to one of the "little colored schools," but that a real college wouldn't take a chance on him.

The final level of trust came when Stanley Easter told us that his family's nickname for him was the Easter Bunny.

"With a last name like Easter," he said, "it was bound to happen. And besides, I was born on April the fourth, which wasn't Easter that year, but close to it."

Stanley also told us that he was very proud of his last name. It had come, he said, because his great-great-grandfather, who was a slave, had actually been born on an Easter Sunday. For people from two different worlds, we did not seem to be that far apart.

At the end of the two-week driving time, all three of us got our certificates, put our names on the list to get a route of our own when school started, and Davey and I said goodbye to the Easter Bunny.

The week before school started I got my assignment, including instructions about when to come to the bus garage to check over and pick up my own bus. I was to drive Bus No. 40, a 1950 International chassis finished as a school bus by Thomas Bus Company in High Point, North Carolina. Already nine years old, this giant old bus was the largest size in use in the county and I was to fill it up, not just once, but four times each morning and afternoon for the coming two school years.

On the scheduled day I eagerly asked Mama to drive me to the school bus garage where I reported in to the chief bus mechanic, Mr. Dale Richardson, who showed me No. 40. The old International had just been repainted bright orange, and on the outside at least, it looked great. Inside it wasn't bad either. The summer before, the bench-seat bottoms and backs had been recovered in brown plastic, and everything else on the inside of the bus was either painted green or plated with chrome.

When I took it over, No. 40 had 81,000 miles on the odometer, which was, in fact, no mileage at all, considering that the engine speed on all North Carolina school buses was governed to keep the bus from ever going faster than thirty-five miles per hour, and, in its entire history, the big engine in this bus had never been revved even halfway to its red-line speed. At this rate, these buses could run forever.

Mr. Richardson showed me all around the bus. He showed me the spare tire and the tire chains, which were both fastened up under the tail end of the big bus. He assured me that I would never need to use either one. If the bus ever did have a flat tire, the garage truck would come and change it, and he said school would always let out in bad weather long before the tire chains were ever needed. "It's just that a few years ago one of the school board members had a tire business and he talked them into buying all of that stuff for the buses. I'll bet he made enough to retire off of that!"

We got in the bus, and I was shown all the controls. I already knew all of this stuff, of course, from the classes, but I listened anyway because Mr. Richardson seemed to be so interested in telling me everything in his own way. He even gave me a new broom, which had had about one-third of the handle sawed off of it to make it easier to sweep the bus with. He told me that he expected me to sweep the bus out every day, and that the garage men would wash the bus once a week and that they would keep the gas filled up and the oil checked.

As I looked around the bus that was to be mine, I noticed the announcement stenciled over the rearview mirror: *Maximum Capacity 92: 78 seated, 14 standing. No Standing Forward of the White Line.* Mr. Richardson saw me looking at the announcement, and he answered the question that must have been on my face.

"Yeah, it'll hold that many. Seventy-eight in the seats—that's thirteen seats on each side with *three* to a seat—then fourteen more standing up in the aisle. If you ask me, you could stand more up than that, but it's hard to fit three in a seat after they get to about the sixth grade. I reckon it all comes out in the wash!" I didn't see what in the world the wash had to do with anything right now.

Mr. Richardson handed me a map of my route and the worn keys—only one set, no allowance for losing them—and then he turned No. 40 over to me. "Take it home today, and in the next day or two take it out and drive over the route. This route's been taking other drivers about an hour and thirty-five minutes to make, so on the first day you ought to be at the first stop by about ten minutes 'til seven."

I started to climb onto the bus, and Mr. Richardson called to me once again. "Oh, Hawk," he wiped his forehead with the back of his hand as he talked, "you'll want to play around a little with the brakes." I looked puzzled. "There's a vacuum booster on the brakes, and the vacuum pressure don't hold real good...there's a gauge on the dashboard you can look at. After you've pulled a long hill, you may not have much for brakes...hit the gas and let off a few times to build it up...you'll catch on to it!"

Even with the warning, the first time I touched the brakes after coasting down the long hill from the bus garage, I almost stood the big bus on its nose. The bus had no seat belts, and I slid out of the seat and right onto the floor under the steering wheel. When I finally looked at the dashboard and found the vacuum gauge, the needle was flat against the MAX post. I would learn to keep my eye on it from now on.

Just after leaving the bus garage on the way from school toward home, I had to pull a long mile-and-a-half hill into the middle of town before coming on through town to our house. Unloaded and with no stops, the big bus pulled the hill at twenty-five miles an hour in third gear. But all the way up the hill, I could see the needle on the vacuum gauge slowly dropping. By the time I got to the Haywood Street stop sign at the top of the long pull, the brake pedal went flat to the floor.

This was no real problem since I was headed uphill. When I pushed the clutch in, the heavy bus stopped on its own, and all I had to do was slip it into first gear the moment it came to its full stop, catch it with the clutch to keep it from rolling backwards, and ride the clutch until traffic was clear and I could pull out and on my way. But I did realize that this might be a problem if you had to go back down a long hill immediately after going up one.

I was fully aware that this was my first time ever to drive a school bus "solo." Mr. Bennett had always been there before. And the 1950 International was somewhat different from the new '59 Chevy we had learned to drive in bus drivers' school. Going over the route could wait until tomorrow; just getting No. 40 home would be enough for me for today.

That night I proudly and conscientiously mopped the inside of the bus, then with a stepladder and a bottle of Glass Wax, I cleaned every one of the windows inside and out. At the Esso station I had even bought an air freshener shaped like a pine tree, and I carefully suspended it from the rearview mirror.

I gave Mama, Daddy, and Joe a tour of the bus, and when Joe asked if he could ride with me the next day when I went over the route, I was mature; instead of saying, "Of course not, are you an idiot?" I politely said, "I'm so sorry, but that would be against the rules."

I studied the route map that night. After breakfast the next day, I took the big bus over the course I would follow well over three hundred times in the next two years.

No. 40 was one of two buses that had routes running from the top of Clyde Valley all the way into town to Sulpher Springs High School. No. 39, the other Clyde Valley bus, started at the top of the valley and came straight down the paved highway, picking up children who gathered themselves into clots about every half-mile along the road.

My bus had what was by far the more interesting Clyde Valley route. No. 40 picked up all of the kids who lived on the half dozen or so dirt roads that ran up and dead-ended in various creekside coves along the sides of the bigger main valley. On these roads, the houses were far apart, and the kids were picked up only one or two at a time.

The beginning of the run was at the top of Wedder's Creek, where the bus had to pull a long two-mile unpaved hill. There was no trouble pulling the hill in second gear with no load on board. I wondered what would happen if we were loaded.

All the way up the long hill I watched the vacuum pressure drop on the dashboard gauge. It was below five pounds when I got to the top. Having driven all these roads in bus driving school, I knew there was a level turnaround place on the right side at the top to back the bus into before going back down the hill.

This was a cinch. All you had to do was wait until the exact moment when the bus stopped, double-clutch it into first gear, and ride the clutch to slow it as you turned the wheel and let it drift gently back into the turnaround place. Once there, the bus was perpendicular to the hillside and it sat still all on its own while I alternately revved the engine and left off the gas until the vacuum gauge came up to ten pounds.

Going down the hill in second gear, the pressure actually kept increasing. Everything was fine as long as I, instead of riding the brake, kept pumping it gently to take advantage of the growing vacuum pressure. I had, I was sure, mastered the system.

It took me just over forty-five minutes to drive the route with no one on board, so I was quite sure I could do it in an hour and a half with all the stopping and starting added in.

Our house had a long concrete driveway that went uphill from the road to the garage. I carefully backed the bus up the driveway and parked it on the grass beside the garage. In cold weather this parking position turned out to be most helpful. Once the temperature dropped below thirty degrees, the old six-volt battery could not muster enough kick to turn the engine over. It was a big help to be able to roll down the driveway with the switch on and then let the clutch out in second gear until at least most of the cylinders were firing by the time you reached the road at the bottom.

I hardly slept on the night before school started. Davey Martin came over to my house, and we talked half the night. He had been given bus No. 22, which went from Gomorrah through Riverside and back.

For the first time since summer we talked about Stanley Easter and wondered if he had gotten a bus route for the year. We decided to try calling Stanley on the telephone to find out, but there were no Easters listed in the Nantahala County telephone book. When we told Daddy what we were doing, he said, "Aw, boys, I don't reckon colored people would have a telephone...especially country colored people." I had never even thought about that before.

The next morning I was up at five-thirty, on the way by six-fifteen, and so far ahead of time that I had to pull off by the side of the road up in Clyde Valley and wait for fifteen minutes so the children at my first stop wouldn't find out that I didn't even know when to leave home. I was ready.

There was one little boy waiting to be picked up at the top of the hill. I would learn later that his name was Hallie Cosby, but on this first day I never found out. I backed the bus into the turnaround place and opened the door, and Hallie Cosby climbed on.

"Good morning!" I said. "I'm your bus driver." Hallie Cosby just stared at me like one of us was from another planet, said nothing at all, and sat down in the seat immediately behind my driver's seat, a position which he was to occupy every time he rode the bus for the next two years.

Later on I was told by the other kids, "Hallie don't talk."

"What do you mean?" I asked them. "Is he deaf or something?"

"He just don't talk," a little girl named Sandra Campbell replied. Arthur Setzer—about a fifth grader, I guessed—offered, "I bet he ain't got no vocal cores!" None of these kids seemed to know why. Actually, nobody seemed to know Hallie well enough to even guess why he didn't talk. The only consensus of agreement was, simply, "Hallie don't talk."

Being an eighth grader, Hallie turned out to be not only the first passenger I picked up each day, he was also one of the few students whom I had on the bus for the entire trip to the combined Sulpher Springs Junior/Senior High School. I did not realize on that first day that I was not simply to haul one load of students to one school; rather, by the time I arrived at the Junior/Senior High School at 8:25, I had moved four loads totaling more than 200 students to four different schools.

During the first seven miles of the route, I picked up a full load of students on three dirt roads, then stopped at Clyde Valley Elementary School. At this point, all of the elementary students got off, while the junior and senior high students stayed on. Now the bus was three-fourths empty again.

As the route went on for the next eight miles, I again filled up the bus and when I now stopped at Mauney Lake Elementary School, about forty elementary students got off and about twenty older students stayed on. From there, the next nine miles, the process was repeated one more time, until when I stopped at Sulpher Springs Elementary in town, only thirty younger students got off and now about sixty junior and senior high students were still on the bus. At this same stop, nearly thirty junior and senior high students, who lived near enough to the elementary school to walk there, boarded No. 40, and the big bus, full for the fourth time, traveled the last three miles to Sulpher Springs Junior/Senior High School, arriving just five minutes before the first bell rang.

I carried out this process as a matter of assumed course and did not realize until years later either the massive responsibility I was, as a sixteen-year-old, carrying out, or the sheer genius of the route-maker who, since I was paid forty-three dollars every twenty days, had me moving pupils to and from school for little more than a penny per student per day!

On the very first day of school, as I made the leg of the run from Mauney Lake School toward Sulpher Springs Elementary, I met another school bus headed in the opposite direction. The bus was as big as No. 40, but older and in need of repainting.

For just a moment I wondered why this strange bus was going in the wrong direction, but as soon as I saw that it was loaded with black children, I knew. This bus was headed for the backside of Nantahala County, headed for tiny Pigeon River School, picking up black children who lived in sight of the same schools I hauled white children to.

As this other bus approached, the driver flashed the headlights, *Flash...flash...flash flash flash*—and I could quickly see that the bus driver was none other than Stanley Easter. He and I both smiled and waved, and from that day on we met, morning and afternoon, on almost the same stretch of road, and flashed our headlights as a silent salute of comradeship with one another.

During the fall football season, there would occasionally be a tiny back-page mention of the Pigeon Eagles football team when they won a game in Black 1-A conference play. Whenever this team was mentioned, Stanley Easter's name was featured as the one who had either led in yards rushing or who had scored the winning touchdown or both. I showed these articles to Mama and Daddy, and Daddy always said, "One of those little colored schools will snap that boy up, sure enough...he's a big'un!"

What I wondered was how Stanley Easter could drive a school bus morning and afternoon and still get in enough time at football practice to not only play but to be the leading scorer, while he was still only in the eleventh grade.

There were great adventures along the way in bus driving. One of the things that I soon discovered was that the route was run much more quickly if you could make the stops as the bus traveled downhill rather than uphill. I discovered this the first afternoon when it took two full hours to undo the same trip I had made in an hour and a half in the morning.

This was the difference: in the mornings, when I stopped to pick up children as the bus traveled down Wedder's Creek road toward school, the heavy bus, after the downhill stop, was almost immediately back up to its thirty-five mile-an-hour maximum speed. But, on that first afternoon, as I let the children off one at a time on the way back up the long hill, I could never even get the bus out of first gear after starting back up, and it crept, roaring and groaning, at about five miles per hour slowly up the hill to the next stop. Two and a half miles of this crawling took over thirty minutes!

I quickly convinced the kids that if they would all sit still as we went all the way to the top of Wedder's Creek without stopping on the way, we could zoom up that hill at fifteen miles an hour in second gear compared to the bare crawl in first if we stopped on the way up. Then I could let them off on the way back down the hill and we would, in this clever way, cut a full twenty minutes off the afternoon trip home.

Because of this new plan, Hallie Cosby, who was the first one onto the bus in the morning, was not the last off in the afternoon. No, all of the kids on the whole long Wedder's Creek hill road rode right past their own houses to the very top with non-talking Hallie. He got off at the turnaround, then the others got off as we went back down the hill.

In about the middle of October, about six weeks into the school year, I arrived at the top of the route one morning and Hallie was not there. I waited for a full five minutes, revving the engine in part to build the brakes up and in part to be sure that Hallie could hear that the bus was there. Finally I was sure he wasn't coming and I started on down the hill, picking up the others, whom I was getting to know pretty well by now.

When I picked up Arthur Setzer, I asked, "Do you know if Hallie's sick or something? He didn't come out this morning!"

Arthur just shyly looked at the floor, seemed to giggle, and didn't give me an answer.

I kept asking other children and kept getting giggles until finally, Sandra Campbell was brave enough to fill me in.

"He's in the hospital," she said. "Broke his leg!"

"Wow," I said. "What happened to him? Did he fall off of something?" The others were all giggling a lot by now.

"Yeah," she said. "He fell through a fence."

What had happened, I finally found out, was that on the Saturday before, Hallie had been helping his daddy and his uncle work a moonshine still, not very far from their house. It seems that Sheriff Tate was out snooping around and found the whiskey still, all fired up, while nobody was there. The sheriff hid out and waited, knowing that the owners would be back soon.

When Hallie and the two men got to the still, Sheriff Tate stepped out, and Hallie's daddy and uncle ran off and left him. "They knew," Sandra explained, "that Hallie couldn't talk and witness against them even if he did get caught." Well, Hallie had tried to run and fell through an old dilapidated fence and broke his leg.

He was out of school another day or so with his leg—and another week, it turned out, because of embarrassment. Then he was back again.

None of us ever had any real discipline problems as student bus drivers. Our instructions were very clear: if we had any trouble on the way home in the afternoon, we were simply to turn the bus around and take everyone all the way back to school. Once back at school, the students would have to call their parents to come to school to get them. Anyone who ever had to go through this once never misbehaved again; the other kids on the bus wouldn't allow it, they all wanted to go home! Of course, there was never any trouble in the mornings because we were, after all, on our way toward school, and the first person to meet the bus at school when we got there was always the principal.

Davey and I now had a wonderful new dimension to our friendship. Almost every day we would call each other when we got home and exchange our adventures of the day. I was a little jealous because he always seemed to have more exciting and daring adventures than I ever had with No. 40.

On Davey's route up through Gomorrah, his run went past a little tourist attraction called Gomorrah Gardens Reptile Center. Locally we all called Gomorrah Gardens "the snake farm." It was a second-class tourist trap that featured big fluorescent-painted plywood road signs, which, for miles in either direction, told you how many miles it was to Gomorrah Gardens. We all knew that the snake farm would pay fifty cents a foot for nonpoisonous snakes and a dollar a foot for deadly ones. We often joked about going out in the mountains to "hunt rattlesnakes and make some money," but we all knew that this was just empty talk.

In addition to many snakes, one caged bear, turkey buzzards in a terrible-smelling cage, and a pair of penned-up wildcats, the snake farm had a half-dozen peacocks and peahens who walked about freely inside the fence.

One afternoon I got home to find the telephone already ringing. It was Davey calling, eager to tell me of his afternoon bus adventure.

"I got a peacock!" he proclaimed. "I got a peacock. Come on over here and I'll give you some feathers!"

I hurried over to his house to hear the great story face to face.

"If I hadn't remembered Mr. Bennett's advice, I might've wrecked the bus!" he said proudly. "I was coming down the dirt road that comes right around the back of the snake farm. I had already let everybody off who lived on that road and was headed back for the paved highway with the last few kids when it happened.

"There must have been a hole in the back fence of the snake farm, and one of those big peacocks just got out. Just as we hit that straight stretch of road, that peacock came right out in the road in front of me, just like it was trying to see if it could get across the road before the bus got there.

"I remembered what happened with Bobby Jensen and that dog so I didn't jerk the wheel or anything. I just held on and went straight ahead and thought, *If it doesn't move, it's dead!* It didn't move."

Davey went on to tell how the few children left on the bus begged to stop and get the feathers they saw flying up in the air as the peacock was hit. They did stop (it was past the summer season and nobody was anywhere around the snake farm right now), and Davey himself came home with fourteen perfect peacock tail feathers—and a promise from the other children not to show theirs to anybody.

"You dummy!" I said. "How is anybody going to hide a peacock feather?" We never did know whether they somehow *did* manage to hide the feathers, or that their parents felt the same way we did about the snake farm and just didn't care. Nothing bad ever came from the peacock business, and I went home with two peacock feathers.

It was a great year, that junior year in high school. Davey and I drove our buses and were closer to being adults than we would ever be again for years to come. We looked forward to our senior year at Sulpher Springs High School, where, once again, the two of us expected to be driving Nos. 40 and 22.

Something happened that summer, however, that changed all that. Davey Martin, my best friend, the friend whom I trusted more than anyone else in the world, went to the bad! Davey Martin fell in love!

The culprit was Sandra Trout, the girl who had kept Davey out late on the great beach trip at Easter. Sandra Trout, whose father was the one surgeon at the Nantahala County Memorial Hospital. Sandra Trout, who lived in a beautiful house and was herself, in a word, beautiful!

Once Davey fell in love, he became totally worthless as a friend. He would rather be "doing something" with Sandra than doing *anything* with the rest of the world. And when he did happen to end up with me, all he did was talk about Sandra, Sandra, Sandra. It was disgusting.

The lowest blow came near the end of the summer. The time came for us to go pick up our school buses for the new year. Mama was planning to give me a ride up to the school bus garage to meet with Mr. Richardson and get No. 40 back for the year. I called Davey on the telephone to see if he wanted to go at the same time.

"Well," he seemed to sound like he was smiling while he told me, "you go on up there and get that old bus. I'm not going to be driving this year. I've got other things to concentrate on...important things!"

I couldn't believe what I heard! It was the last straw.

As it turned out, giving up the bus route was not entirely Davey's own idea. It seems that his life had been taken over not only by Sandra Trout but also by her parents, especially her surgeon father, Dr. Trout.

Sandra's father had gone to Harvard, and everyone in town knew it. It was almost impossible for anyone to ever have a conversation with Dr. Trout without at some point having to hear the words, "When I was at Harvard..." followed by a school story. His Harvard diploma hung right on the wall, not in his private office, but right out in the reception room where it was hard not to see it (though most residents of Nantahala County, not being able to read Latin, had no idea what the big framed certificate was all about).

When I talked to Davey about a week after school started, the real plan for his life came out. We were just beginning to talk about applying for colleges for the next year when everything suddenly became clear to me.

"Dr. Trout says," Davey began, "that nobody born in Nantahala County has ever been admitted to Harvard. He says that he doesn't even think that anybody from Nantahala County has ever even applied."

I was carefully listening now, for what I knew was coming next.

"Dr. Trout says that with his coaching and a lot of hard work, he thinks that maybe I could get accepted and that if somebody from a place as remote as this ever got accepted, they would have to give him a scholarship. That's the real reason I'm not going to drive a bus this year. I'm going to work for Dr. Trout in the lab at the hospital after school and on some Saturdays, and he's going to help me with my schoolwork and coach me through applying to Harvard."

"Harvard?" I couldn't believe it. "What in the world is wrong with you? You don't have any business even thinking about something like that. It's that girl, isn't it? That doctor's got you married already and he's going to be ashamed of you if he can't take over your life and make you into something he wants you to be."

Davey looked so much like he had been slapped that I knew I had, even if by pure accident, stumbled close to the truth. "Why doesn't he send his own daughter to Harvard? Don't they take women?"

"I honestly don't know…if they take women, that is. Sandra wants to go to some girls' school up there close, and Dr. Trout really thinks that this is a good idea."

And so the tone of the year was set. Davey, Sandra, and Dr. Trout spent every available moment together, with Dr. Trout single-handedly planning the future for all of them. I, with no best friend, having spent all of last year with either Davey or No. 40, began the process of applying to Davidson College, an old North Carolina school which was surely as far from home as I had any business trying to go.

No. 40 occupied almost all of my free time and energy. I did play in the Sulpher Springs High School band, but that was mostly a weekend commitment. From before daylight until the edge of dark, I contented myself with the company of silent Hallie Cosby, and Sandra Campbell and Arthur Setzer, now a year older and wiser, as well as over two hundred more just like them. And, yes, I kept waving to Stanley Easter morning and afternoon, though my recollection of the friendship we had started in bus driving school was only the very palest of memories.

In February I was accepted to Davidson College and began to watch Mama make her own plans for my departure. And lo and behold, in March, it was Dr. Trout who announced that "Davey Martin has just become the first person ever born in this county to be accepted at Harvard University for the class of 1965." He didn't even mention that his own daughter had, all on her own, applied to and been accepted at Wellesley—a place none of us had ever heard of at the time anyway. I guessed that this was the end of the road for Davey and me.

It was in April that the most wonderful and memorable event of my entire bus driving career happened. In fact, it was perhaps the most memorable event of my entire high school career. It all started when, in the middle of a school day, I got sick at school.

It was in the middle of Mrs. Turner's senior English class last period of the afternoon. I had been feeling flush all day, and was beginning to get a little bit woozy, when, all of a sudden, without notice, I felt a wave of nausea that was so quick and so powerful that there was not even time to ask for permission to leave the room. I simply ran for the door, knowing that my illness would cover every excuse I needed later. I barely made it to the bathroom and was losing several meals at once when Davey, whom Mrs. Turner sent to "find out whatever is going on with that young man," came in and saw the problem. He left me and went back to report to Mrs. Turner.

When Davey returned to the bathroom to see what he could do for me, I realized that there was no way I could drive No. 40. "Go to the bus garage," I begged, "And tell Mr. Richardson what happened...I can't drive that bus!"

As things finally turned out, Mama came to school to pick me up, and Davey, not driving a bus of his own this year, agreed with Mr. Richardson to be my temporary substitute driver for No. 40.

Thinking about all of this later, I am still certain that I had, at one time or another, told Davey about how long hills depleted the vacuum pressure for the brake booster. With hindsight, I also wondered how he had not figured the brakes out for himself on the first part of the route. But either information was lacking, or Davey's brain was elsewhere (probably with Sandra Trout), or, as he insisted, something mechanical really did go wrong.

Davey got to the top of Wedder's Creek hill, pushed in the clutch, and gravity stopped the big bus. He slipped the bus out of gear, turned the wheel to the right, and No. 40 obediently rolled back to the right into the turnaround place. As it came to a stop, on its own, Davey took advantage of the last movement to turn the big non-powered steering wheel to the left. In that moment everything started to go wrong.

As Hallie Cosby got up from his seat to come to the door to get off, the big orange bus started rolling forward, with—unknown to my friend, substitute driver, and future Harvard student—the vacuum gauge flat on zero.

Davey put his foot on the brake, and the pedal went flat to the floor as No. 40, now with a mind of her own, rolled faster and faster with every passing moment.

If Davey Martin had ever pumped the brake pedal just once, or if he had even let up on it enough to take advantage of the now-increasing downhill vacuum pressure, everything would have been fine. But, in sheer panic, his foot was now frozen to the floor, and instead of pumping, he just tried to push even harder against the floorboard. It didn't work. The big bus didn't even pretend to slow down. Davey held it in the road but had no hopes of making it safely to the bottom of the mountain.

All of a sudden someone was yelling. "Hit dem pines, wild man! Hit dem pines! Hit dem pines, wild man! Hit dem pines!"

Everyone in the bus stared in silent disbelief as Hallie Cosby, making the first audible sounds anyone had ever heard come from him, jumped up and down in the aisle of the bus beside the driver's seat and pointed to a soft-looking grove of hemlock bushes located along the right side of the road not fifty yards ahead.

Davey later admitted that there was not enough time to actually think through a decision. Maybe his brain did remember the driver's class bus sinking slowly into the soft cornfield when Bobby

Jensen went for the dog, and maybe not. Whatever thought process went on, the "pines" did seem to be the softest and safest thing to run into before the bus gained enough speed to be totally out of control, and so, Davey did indeed "hit dem pines"!

No. 40 slowed as it plowed through the young hemlocks, came out on the other side, and landed softly in the shallow mire where Hallie's daddy and uncle dumped the spent mash from the moonshine still they had hidden there. Running the big bus into a pillow couldn't have provided a softer landing. Most of the dozen riders still left on the bus didn't even fall out of their seats throughout the whole crash landing.

I later realized that the worst thing about being sick on that day was that I was not able to go up to Wedder's Creek to see my drunken bus before it was pulled out of the mash-mire.

Hallie didn't say a word after the bus came to its safe stop. He just got off the bus, waded out of the mash, and walked home, as did the other kids still left on the bus.

The next day Mr. Poindexter, the principal, called Hallie into the office for a conference about the entire bus business.

"Hallie," Mr. Poindexter started off, "we didn't even know you could talk. Why hadn't you ever said anything before yesterday afternoon?"

Hallie's reply was simple. "They wadn't never nothing needed saying." And that was that.

No. 40 was not hurt at all by the drunken trip through the hemlocks, and in just a few days both of us were back on the road again. The orange bus did, though, have an interesting odor for the rest of the year. And Davey Martin, my former best friend, the boyfriend of Dr. Trout's daughter, now accepted to enter Harvard as a freshman in September, never drove another school bus again.

We graduated on the fourth day of June, 1961. I told the old bus goodbye. Never in my life would I again have another job that involved such actual responsibility as this job had. Davey and I spent our summers getting ready in our own separate ways to say goodbye to Sulpher Springs and, finally, to one another.

In September, Davey Martin, loaded up in Dr. Trout's latest Buick station wagon, left for Massachusetts. He was headed for his date with destiny, all planned by his girlfriend's father. I packed up, with Mama's help, and went on my more proper way to Davidson College, in the flatlands of the same state in which I had been born and always lived.

Before my first day at freshman orientation was over, I knew that I was in a different world. It was 1961 and this was a Southern, male-only, liberal arts school for the white and well-cultivated sons of the South. As I abandoned my blue jeans and flannel shirt and quickly bought a yellow Gant shirt and Bass Weejuns so I would at least appear to fit in, I knew that there were many things about my mountain childhood that I would not only leave behind but about which I would positively lie to cover up my uncultured upbringing.

One of the things I would never admit to my sophisticated freshman classmates was my history as a North Carolina school bus driver. As I realized this, I chuckled to myself, knowing how many more things Davey Martin would try to cover up in order to be accepted up at Harvard. I began to live out a fresh, clean—if somewhat revised from reality—personal history.

We were fresh in the first year of what was to be the brief presidency of John F. Kennedy. The hottest elective course open to freshmen on campus was a political science course called "Current Politics: The Pulse of Washington." I signed up for the course, partly because it sounded interesting and partly because it offered a Thanksgiving trip to Washington. I was in such a ripe mood to get away from home that this prospect sounded great to me.

Mama cried on the telephone when I told her that I wouldn't be home for Thanksgiving. In the middle of my attempt to explain my desire to "broaden my horizons," she kept talking about "forgetting where you came from." It was with a mixture of feelings that my first trip to our nation's capital drew near.

The political science class went up on a chartered bus on Wednesday afternoon. I felt like the king of the world as we came over the last ridge in Virginia and looked down on the Pentagon and on across to the city of monuments, now lighted in the darkness of our night arrival.

We were staying in dormitory rooms at American University, rooms emptied by students who had gone home for this holiday. There were students from other visiting colleges staying in the same dorm. They were, we discovered, there for the same reason we had come.

We were left to wander on our own on Thanksgiving Day, and it was then that my Davidson roommate and I met up with the boys from Harvard. They were staying in the dormitory room next to where we were staying, and after forming a quick friendship, the four of us decided to go to the Washington Monument and then get a pizza together.

All four of us talked about college and about Washington and about politics and about John Kennedy, just like we knew what we were talking about. We waited in line in a stiff wind that blew all around the Washington Monument until, after an hour, we rode to the top and then walked back down. Then it was off to get a bite to eat.

At the pizza parlor, one of the Harvard boys said, "Where are you guys from?"

"Davidson College," I answered quickly. "You-all know that."

"That's not what I mean," the new Harvard friend went on. "Where are you *really* from? Like, where did you grow up?" It was the awful question that I did not at all want to deal with in front of these new, sophisticated friends.

I tried to get off with a generically vague answer. "North Carolina."

The Harvard questioner persisted. "What part?"

I was not about to say "Sulpher Springs." At the time that was the stupidest place in the world I thought anybody could be from—so stupid the name was even spelled wrong. After a long pause, I finally said, "Close to Asheville." It was as close to the truth as I was going to get.

"Close to Asheville?" one of them asked. "Is it anywhere close to a place called *Sulpher Springs?*"

My heart almost stopped! Where in the world did they hear about Sulpher Springs?

The other one chimed in. "Yeah! We've got a classmate from Sulpher Springs, North Carolina. He's the coolest guy you ever met. You know what? He says he drove a school bus in high school! Isn't that about the coolest thing you've ever heard of?"

All my fears melted. So Davey had not lied about where he came from, and these guys really didn't think that Sulpher Springs, North Carolina, was stupid after all. All of a sudden I felt terribly home-sick, and Nantahala County was the only place in the world that seemed worth talking about. I swelled with pride.

"Well," I started in, "you won't believe this, but I am from Sulpher Springs too, and I also drove a school bus, and that classmate of yours is my very best friend in all the world. We grew up together and we even got our bus drivers' licenses at the same time!"

"Oh, yeah!" They were really talking now. "He told us all about bus driver's school. Did that guy really chase after that dog with a school bus and end up in a cornfield? That's the funniest thing I ever heard!"

"It sure did happen." I was loving this. "It happened just the way he told you. It was the funniest thing you've ever seen in your life. You should have seen the farmer when he came running out of his house and saw the bus."

We were all laughing. "So you were best friends, huh?"

"I guess we still are," I went on. "Say, did he ever tell you about running my school bus into a hole full of moonshine mash? Now that was really the funniest."

The two of them looked at each other. "No," one of the Harvard boys shook his head. "We never heard of that."

"You mean"—I was laughing on my own now, just remembering the whole story—"he didn't tell you about having no brakes, and about dumb Hallie Cosby, who had never spoken a word in his life yelling, 'Hit dem pines, wild man,' and saving the bus?"

They were still looking blank and shaking their heads. *So,* I thought, *old Davey didn't tell everything! I'm going to let the cat out of the bag!*

"You mean," I laughed, "that Davey Martin didn't tell you that he wrecked my school bus?" I waited for their response.

"Davey Martin?" one of the Harvard boys asked. "Who's Davey Martin? The guy we're talking about is Stanley Easter. Calls himself the Easter Bunny. He's the smartest guy in the freshman class...made over fifteen hundred on his SATs...he's on a full academic scholarship!"

After a moment of dead silence, which was accompanied by a whole lifetime of thoughts and attitudes rearranging themselves in my head, the other Harvard freshman added, almost as an afterthought, "There is a Davey Martin in our class...but he says he's from 'up above Atlanta.'"

Seen and heard on CNN, *Nightline,* and American Public Radio's *Good Evening,* DONALD DAVIS has also told stories for audiences throughout the U.S. and in the British Isles, New Zealand, and Indonesia. His other books include a novel, a children's picture book, two collections of stories, and two instructional books on writing and storytelling. An award-winning recording artist, he has received the Parents' Choice Gold Award, *Audiofile's* Earphones Award, *Storytelling World's* Best Audiotape Award, and a Notable citation from the American Library Association. He lives on Ocracoke Island off the North Carolina coast.

OTHER BOOKS BY DONALD DAVIS

Many of Davis's stories are also available on audio cassette and CD.

Listening for the Crack of Dawn

A Master Storyteller Recalls the Appalachia of the '50s and '60s
His first and best-loved book, this collection includes school stories
"Winning and Losing," "Miss Daisy," and "Experience" as well as
eleven additional stories relating Davis's childhood
amongst his family, school, and community.
Paperback ISBN 0-87483-605-0

See Rock City

A Story Journey Through Appalachia
A recounting of more of Davis's Appalachian upbringing,
this sequel to *Listening for the Crack of Dawn* consists of eleven
stories, including "Mrs. Rosemary" and "Stanley Easter."
Hardback ISBN 0-87483-448-1 / Paperback ISBN 0-87483-456-2

Barking at a Fox-Fur Coat

Family Stories and Tall Tales
Stories and tall tales from Davis's own family,
guaranteed to keep you laughing into the next generation.
Hardback ISBN 0-87483-141-5 / Paperback ISBN 0-87483-140-7

Southern Jack Tales

Jack, the Appalachian Everyman, confronts difficulties common to
all cultures with courage and wit in these traditional mountain tales.
Paperback ISBN 0-87483-500-3

Thirteen Miles from Suncrest

Davis recreates a simpler time in this novel of
early 1900s life in rural Close Creek, North Carolina.
Hardback ISBN 0-87483-379-5 / Paperback ISBN 0-87483-455-4

Writing as a Second Language

From Experience to Story to Prose
In this non-fiction resource for language teachers and
beginning writers of all ages, Davis sets forth a step-by-step
writing process that begins with the spoken word.
Paperback ISBN 0-87483-567-4

AUGUST HOUSE PUBLISHERS, INC.
1-800-284-8784 • P.O. Box 3223, Little Rock, AR 72203 • www.augusthouse.com